DEREK MCKEWAN

TIME EPIC

LIFE. KNOWLEDGE. FUTURE

CAST OF CHARACTERS

Lightermann (formerly "Vandergaard")
Grey Fox - changeling/ werewolf, Navajo Apache, 1800 pounds of pure muscle
Eiko-superfast/supersmart, super-inventor
I. Victorian- female Brit

Herkomar-their leader, speaks over 20 languages
Herkomar's daughter
Constiglione
Hanna
Lc vay
Alexia
Spade (an American)

+2 or 3 additional others.

CHAPTERS

1670s-the study involving muskets, age of piracy, visit to Spain, England

Late 1680s-on colonialism, currency, and they settle on america

1690s-the argument over the printing press, and the introduction of spade

Modern Period (late Colonial)

1700s (the first decade)-the article on hemp, and their stay in america

1720s-Lightermann goes to college, and also, Catherine the Great I

Late 1730s-the meetup with Grey Fox, and the article on spade

1770s-Hanna, the older mage female, takes exit

1790s-I Victorian builds an evening club

After Enlightenment Period

1820s-Napoleanic Wars, I Victorian gets knighted

1830s-invasion of Algeria, Brussels

1840s-the publication of Leif Sterling, and a friend of theirs, constiglione, perishes close to Alaska

1850s-the story about Herkomar, in which he spends time with a female acquaintance, and their third tour of france

1860s-an additional scene with alexia.

1870s-their version of a Western, with Grey Fox; and lightermann goes back to college

1880s-the story about Pakistan; the camera invention, and Herkomar meets another woman

Late 1880s-the discovery of Eiko, in which he proposes theory of immortality

1890s-herkomar reads the time machine, and introduces studies in time travel, with I Victorian

-220 B.C.-Victoria and Herkomar in Rome

INTRODUCTION PROLOGUE-THE DARK AGES (1440?)

(written by Hanna; later revised by Hanna, in 1634) (tells story of earlier race of immortals, who apparently she killed)

Okay, to start off, for one, I did not vanish Alexia. I know that Herkomar, in his mindset, would of course not believe me. However, I feel I should at least say that much. Alexia disappeared. We know not where.
-Hanna

The purpose of this intro, is partially, as Herkomar intended, and requested of me, to be for illuminated entertainment, and also, for record, and also for somewhat, historical value. I. Victorian was, of course a Brit. Constiglione was at least Italian. Herkomar was, of course, *switzer*. Later, he described himself as being German, for sorts of various political reasons of his own. These, with myself of course, configured, the original group for entering the new Renaissance. We named ourselves the Trinity. Constiglione was our fourth.

And with that appended, I further cast.

We guided towards the sun quite often. Some days we got there quicker. This is not very funny, someone insists.

Then, I'll have to check with my main records *book*, says I.

They good-hearted well-esteemed well-educated erudite classes say, we are all here, brought forth by recognition.

And also, to my above decent well holding, that which it is, to say, surely focused and correctly maintained, these actual facts, three, and events, are clear, and crisp, and sharp, and notice.

My name is Hanna.

Some say in legends, I descended from Rome.

Earlier historians have placed me more correctly, as being Norwegian.

When Herkomar and I found and founded this group, there were only three. Me, myself, Herkomar and Victorian, as mentioned. We found ourselves a trio, and we added our fourth member later. The other two were already there.

A few notes about Victorian. Her real name was Lady *I*. Victorian. Victorian was sort of a trashy, pompous example of a female arts mage -hyph- warrior princess; if you wanted to ask me about her. She liked to smoke, and she liked to fight. Herkomar's crowning achievement, she always bragged. She thought this was a brag, but I knew it wasn't a good one. Proper tastes and all.

To tell, Some days I felt I couldn't stand Victorian at all. But she was a friend of Herkomar, and for that reason I never said anything. It was no big deal. She was founded in 1263, in the highest of Upper London, and cited in basically two years after the Spanish Inquisition.

I guess we were one of the meaner groups, after all.

Herkomar, as he called himself, "Herkomar the Best", was born to a royal family, as well, in 1108. This was somewhere around the swiss mountains back when. If you were alive back then, you'd know the way I was talking. He hunted, and used bow and long sticks. As a soldier in the hundred year war, he was known to be quite, and very, exceptional. For, He had always found himself to be one of the best, and the best and the best at the age of forty. He, himself, looks only thirty, even nowadays. At time of writing, it is when-about 1441 or 1443, and possibly a good few years after that.. Drinking, he did not always conduct ever. We found him for that reason. -Hnna

Great wealth came with nobility, which was how we could always afford. Constiglione made his money off inventory. We earliest encountered him mid-1300s. Selling off mid-large parts of iron metal sheeting, to protect from the warm in some areas, we guessed. Later, he made his fortune.- Hnna
And there was more than that.

Also.
Two, interesting notes: The assumption that I was born in Rome had to do with another predate. Earlier, before Herkomar and the rest came into being, founding or being, founding or being, there was a race of others, an earlier race of Immortals such as mine and mine own. We were from another class.

I nearly killed them all, for they were cruel-minded, and barbaric. Four of them, I ordered to have them burned alive. Three of them I murdered with my own bare hands. You thought I was about say I extinguished only two. No. I killed three of them. With my bare hands, as mentioned. And the rest of them, as well, I killed them too, or ordered, I did, to have them assassinated, they were so intolerably atrocious and despicable.

I won't say I felt bad about this. I live in a temple nowadays. Basically.

I had murdered the earlier part of my non-Norwegian, non-italian race, as an early Immortal.

Later, after, they were all in the ground, I worried far less for the countryside.

Reciting this story to Herkomar, he of course inquired.

Once, His question: Why would you do something like that, Hanna? Why would you do anything at all like that, Hanna? Why would you kill this older race of immortals, whose existence, of course benefited the great grand world, as Herkomar's did. With their glory and their beauty and their luxuriance, I always figured that he most likely surmised.

To which I replied, justified, as usual: They were evil.

Now, Herkomar, and of course if you know Herkomar, would still debate. Those who knew him, all knew he was always, *always* convinced of greater good and greater value. He refused my answer, as he would. That's what I would always come to love about him. To that, he actually believed. The H-Razors of Nine Circ., he must've thought, could not have been that bad. For If he actually knew the actual name of the group, and what sorts of evil they would actually conduct, he would probably have a miniature heart attack right in front of me, they were so evil and despicable.

Yet still, in his conversation.

Herkomar's reasoning: That all immortals are important. That all immortal entities, should be awarded to a chance.

I asserted, as later, he awarded LeVay, and I reminded him of the results.

The story of LeVay has been included in Herkomar's book, for a very important reason. And a practical one. For a few, it represents

a journey of meet, and, to others, the ultimate quest in quest jour-
neying. However. For me, I thought LeVay was just another item of
crack underworth. He had to be taken out, like all the others, in the
end. To say that, I Hanna, would have gladly killed him too.

Must've forgotten, I'd say.

All evil must be destroyed.

Your Good Lady Fair,
Hanna

PART I

The Renaissance

The Renaissance

1500s(the first decade)-I. Victoria steals a market
1500s(the first decade)-Breakfast with Herkomar
1520s-Constiglione buys a house
1540s-???
1550s-story of levay (and alexia)
1570s-purported rumor that Hanna has killed Alexia
1580s-Hanna does a demonstration on keys
1590s-discovery of lightermann

1

THE 1500S (THE FIRST DECADE)

I. Victoria steals a market; Constiglione gets harassed, sort of

These notes contain my recollections. Vaguely, these notes should illustrate what good life, on a very typical night, was actually like for all of us, in the early years of the 1500s. I have included this chapter for that reason, and numerous reasons.

-Herkomar

Roughly translated to English, and modernized:

It was, for us, the Coming of New Ages. The time, and greater of new pinnacles, with stunning forms and high brand artistry.

All among, we had dressed very fashionably. That, for us, we seemed to be entering the brighter years of our freshly remarkable lives to greater whole, to greater appeal, and with greater successes, and, for many, to celebrate the coming of the Great New Century, at highest, spectacular grand monument.

Gone was the spiritual haze, that some had noted, in previous decades. We all felt better, more improved, well enhanced, and the newer century was there to lead us forwards.

Your beloved narrator. Herkomar, as my friends call me, sat beside the Royalty. I had been invited to the Grand Ball, for that night, at the House of Royal Magistrates, in Venice, Venice 1502.

Accompanying me, would be the Great I. Victorian, the woman that Hanna had described slightly in her intro notes. Hanna, I felt could've done better justice for such a good-looking woman.

So here,
Lady Victorian, as I had known her well, was a very slender yet full-figured woman, partially blonde, yet still she treated her hair. Jet, at certain times she had dyed it, the color of black quite regularly. And also: She had truly amazing great legs and a notably perfect vanilla white complexion. She often worked out, very well, and wore expensive silk outfits, tightly, and over her voluptuous, yet tightly slender, good looking form

I was, as of that point, over three hundred and twenty years old. Victorian, they say, had lived over two-twenty. She had always been incredibly gorgeous. And incurably magnificent, as well, was the thought on that.

In circles, I still pass for a young man, maybe around thirty or twenty-nine. Later I aged slightly, however still unnoticeably.

Also, then, there was Constiglione, db. 1257.

He had made us a good deal of influence coin off some repair equipment he had been working on. Some of his art suppliers had worked well, and he had brought in a new level of fortune for him and his trade.

At that point he had employed at least eight or nine models working for him all at once, and he crafted great objects and object tricks and also devices in his spare time to build higher grand. I had known Constiglione for a while, and what he was up to.

For a while, he would go to work in Arabia. Some say he was part of the original.

At the ball he was to wear blue black, and also pure white, and a subtle degree of red, to which he did, to represent a formal and informal, slightly guarded, good-looking casual gentleman scholar type. Which, he was, the women had noted. Also, he was known as quite an inventor. Women saw him as a playboy.

His date to the Grand Ball was Lady Sara.

My date to the ball was the lovely stunning I. Victorian, and also I was to take a second or third woman, a very good-looking young red brown-haired model, whose loose name roughly translated to Snow Princess, or Snow Princess, in the Fall.

Before: Our tickets had arrived by female courier. Hanna was invited as well, but she, as center general, declined. Hanna and I referred to us, the rest of us, as: The Trinity. The rest of us; we knew we'd have to show there anyway.

Later: At the first, our passage through Church. I dropped by, and had an early communion. Constiglione dropped off a packet, and we thanked them, very pleasant.

That night of The Evening Ball itself had turned out to be

somewhat pivotal as an event night for We. When Lady Victorian bought the market, she had mentioned this to me, this then.

"I stole the market," she confessed, when we were alone on the balcony.

My real date Snow princess was busy trying to make out with some good looking Spanish guy, I heard about that later at the grand ball.

"How'd you get it?" I asked Victorian.

The Great Market Luciano's had been up for auction for the past two and a half years. Sadly, no one could make a high enough payment for it. Victorian's story was that she simply paid the watchman at the claims house to write three deeds out to her and one of which was for the market, which she admitted later that she bought fair and square, for an agreed upon much lower price. She only paid apparently less than twenty thousand for it, she said. Used her good intelligence to gain some influence, on the dealing maybe, I guess.

"Did you mention this to Hanna?"

"Sure. Not." she answered. "She wouldn't care. She'd probably say so."

"Well, that's the way it goes, I know."

Victorian forked over my portion. A set of keys, with the fancy gold I. Insignia.

Thank you, Lady I..

Constiglione had a share of keys too, but he was busy with an altercation.

Some might wonder why this was important. Trust me, it's very important.

I. Victorian had seized a very, very large amount of grounds

property for an extremely dangerously low, low amount of currency, or trust.

As described, Constiglione was, in the meantime, trapped in an altercation with a group of three men. They looked like loading men to a large extent. The fight was over Lady Sara, at the time, I thought.

Later I got the real story from him. There was a man, apparently he was a highly influential Christian count, looking to pay Constiglione a good thirty-eight or so to involve himself in a profitable land or bank deal operated by their accountancy firm. Constiglione looked around twenty six or twenty eight. The Count might have thought him a good choice.

For truth, he said he slightly balked.

"Did you accept?" I asked him.

"Maybe, maybe I did," was his answer. "He asked again later that night. And I did."

For what purpose? was this. This incident earlier was actually all very important for me to mention, as well.

I explained that Constiglione was a very involved individual. He was known to tell the truth generally always.

The following is very critical, esteemed information:

There was a kindly group, known as the Consortium, that was very, very interested in Constiglione. Whether they knew or not about his involvement with our cadre, noted as The Trinity, mine and Hanna's, was not known. Maybe I suspected they did know this, in fact.

Surely, I was still worried a little.

However...,
For the rest of the decade, and for the rest of next decade, tight operations went moderately very well. And other events. Over the years and years, we still got better. Decade after decade, quality improved.

Together, we focused and evolved. Our businesses skyrocketed. The Trinity became a new success all over again.
There was cash to be made, and we had earned it all.

The world pieced together, for all of us.

There was a period of strife in the background, but however, it seemed to breeze past us, Lady Victorian, Hanna, me, and Constiglione.

We were items without pain. The New Immortals. And we celebrated, and did better for it.
For a very, very long, long while, it seemed.
Until the next business.

1509, there was a minor strike. And that was all.

2

THE 1500S (THE FIRST DECADE)

(more)-Breakfast with Herkomar, in which he reads a poem,

1505. I wake up and procure breakfast.

I eat a good fried steak, along with some leftover breadsticks.

The wind seemed to turn well.

And then I went out, to check on the morning dew.

A young woman makes eye contact. Very attractive.

The New Century has arrived appreciably. That we thought.

Some worked on painting new artistic sets, and some higher quality sets, and newer quality devices.
What a glorious time, was manned.

For a while, I focused on procuring more goods.
Some very high quality built luxury items, were purchased.

I am built like a man.
-Herkomar

And then I stand forward.

1516. We all make a living.

3

THE 1520S

Constiglione buys a house

Four years later.

What someone may be wondering, especially Hanna, I bet, is, why the F' did Herkomar's book just zoom forward over ten or eighteen years into the future. To this, I do not offer fig. To Hanna, I do not listen sometimes.

For a while, Vi had spent four years on the road back in England. Rough for her, over the news. When she returned home to us there was a slight ruckus over the market she bought. On her opinion. And over and over again.

She considered it good, for her. Luciano's proved a profit.

Hanna picked up at the meeting we held over it.

We reasoned, we'd wait a few, draft, and see what held, for the result hand quick later.

The years went by. I'd spent a lot of nights at the betting fair. I met another woman named Alice. Some days, we'd tour all the

Great Markets together.

The metropolis high tested fully in the wares quite often. The citizens, all seemed destined to go forwards.

And, Afterwards.

And, By the way, I have entitled this chapter "Constiglione buys a House." I intended this book for non-selfish reasons, and for some rationale, I am compelled to give another. When it comes to across, a series of vignettes.

We are the spirit alive, said Hanna.
More too, than that.

For a while, we made our investments. Over the years, wealth highly accumulated.
I am merely illustrating this.

And.
By now,
Seeing,
I had mentioned all our names,
and that.
That, by 1520, they say, we had all lived safely again, once again, in Venice.
Our main purpose, was to track and to document, the nature of being of those who had perpetuated to be life, and life immortals.

Technology is a root.

In 1516, Machiavelli had already constructed *The Prince*.

By 1518. Martin Luther had tacked up his posters on reform.

These events meant something.

1521.
We all worked hard. We all worked fierce, on capital.

Some days, our newer champions proved worthy, as well.

Sometime around the 1526, I received a messenger call.

"What do you want?" I asked.
"Simply a time," the messenger in black responded.
"It seems a little after noon." I guessed.
"That sounds fine." He handed over his note. And left.

Wanted, in February,
It read, in large black letters.
A three of four,
A had of nine.
Be-seeing you.
-V

Apparently a threat I figured. Still unsure.
I crawled back on the cotting, and turned over.

Hanna awoke me two hours later. She shook me gently.
"Hanna,"
"Herk...," she said softly. "Herk..."

"Hanna," I said.

"Herk....," softly, "Herk..."

"Are we to go to yet another tea house today?"

"Yes. Chai. Later. You're wanted at the lecture hall right now."

"Shuuuhhh...."

"No," she silenced me. She went over to pick up her well notice. "Let's go," she said.

The streets were all of rainy dew that day.
We walked along the awnings, side.
Me and my blazer. I sure loved that blazer.
It was a long, long longer night last night.

A girl in the street level made a sign at me.
"Thank you," I said.
"Thank you." I said.
And she said, Thank you, very much, and she signed back with her hands.

At the office in Venice, we worked.

There were a bunch of whistles in our direction. Someone good-looking had probably entered the room. I had hoped it was me, but probably it was a woman.

I guessed that was fine.

The men grumbled.

"Your documents and cause...," someone said.

"Sounds solid. Sounds solid," said a younger gentleman, in his mid-twenties. "I looked it over, it sounds solid." He said. He said it again.

I listened carefully, and attentive. We had done several favors. The men had acknowledged this.

They met with a tight group after that. One of the smarter good men made a nod.
Sure. Sure. Said, "We looked over the issue of entitlement, and we think you're in the right."

And that was it. The decision had been worked in our favor. Apparently another route had been established.
Strong.

And eventually that's what became of it.
We had decided to grant Constiglione a third large building. Included with, was a much larger studio. And that is what he deserved.
He had purchased it for over eleven grand.
Someone insisted.

"Constiglione," I asked.
"Yes."
"Constiglione, what's the research?"
"Profitable. It'll take at least fourteen years out of the country."
"Good. That's great."
"They thought they located a buzzyard."
"That's good."

"Do you know what that means?"
"More money for us?"
Yeah.

Later...

Pause.
"Is Vi still in trouble...?"
"Sort of. They're willing to overlook."
"She is pretty, right?"
"Of course." He didn't smile.
"Of course. Of course." I added.
"She didn't realize, they said."
I put my hand over my head, lightly. "Fine. Fine. That's right. Keep me updated," I said.

And Later...

Pause.
"They found something out though."
"What, what though?"
Pause.
"LeVay," he said.
"What?"
"LeVay."
"What? What?"
"LeVay."
"Who the f' is Levay?" I finally asked him.
Pause. Long pause.

"Do you know who I'm talking about?" he questioned.
"No. No, I have no idea who you're talking about."
"Then never mind. Don't mention any of this to Hanna."
I passed over what he said. Then took a cigarette.

We went out for dinner with Hanna later.

"How's Alice?" she asked me.
"Fine. She's just fine."

End of chapter.

4

THE 1540S

Intrigue in Venice,

1545. That decade Constiglione proved to be even more productive. For the year, he invented at least two very unique and clever devices.

The first was a double clock that ran double quadruple speed forward, clockwise, and additionally, also counter-clockwise. This device was later separately invented as the chronograph in 1810, and later, as the stopwatch, in the early part of the twentieth century.

Constiglione's version was slightly off by three or four seconds, per minute sometimes. He often argued to me it was an early draft prototype. Which I believed, although he never made a second one. A very unique early model though, we all thought.

The second device that Constiglione developed for that year, was a Y-shaped crossbow that could apparently hurl large glass bottles over very great distances.

"How long did it take you to make this?" I asked him.

"Slightly over two weeks", was his answer. How very clever, I thought.

One time, while practicing with the crossbow, I accidentally launched an empty bottle of Arlot De' Faire on top of a next door neighbor's white-pink sunset roof. We had been testing with the prototype outside Constiglione's studio. CRASH, it went. The neighbor didn't seem to notice at the time. but later I was harshly scolded about the incident anyway, by an older woman whose name I've mentioned before, but whose name I don't want to mention here right now. Probably I'll mention her at some other point, in this chapter. I had been very angry at Hanna, for a good portion of this decade, over a situation incurred at a dinner party in 1541. And other things.

Later, Constiglione re-developed his crossbows, so that they could also hurl steak knives and other small mid-sized wood stick implements with astonishing relative accuracy. Good work, of course, and very, very innovated.

He marketed some of these as specially manufactured collector's items, for around 230 gold florins apiece, and sold maybe eighty of them their first week on the market.

The days rushed by. Life, and businesses, in the 40s, seemed very much viable.

I relaxed on the evening desk. I practiced with a sword for a while.

Certain times I felt certain subtle pegns of sorrow. Alice had left me more than a decade ago.

I still remember our last fight.

She wanted to go out with me for dinner one night.
I accused her of cheating on me, and then she kicked me out.

We all find new habits, right?

On the streets I walked with Lady Victorian some days. We'd shop for items and cloth trinkets, and things to buy, as well.

However, at certain points in the 40s, I still became suspicious.

At one moment:
Victorian paused. "What's the deal?", she asked.
I said nothing.
We stopped walking. Someone was following us, I felt. Straight, to the back, about twenty meters off.
He wore a large dark costume, complete with an oversized cape.
"What's the matter?" she asked again.
"Vi.?"
"Uh huh."
"Shush."
She looked back. It seems the individual was gone, I bet.
"There's no one there," she said. Tenderly. We quickly moved our street.

For a moment, she could tell that I wanted to cry.

"Did I..? Did I..?"

"Do you care to repeat that, Herkomar?"

"I had one of our couriers make a transaction for us, I thought," I mentioned, to her.

"With whom?"

"Someone. Never mind."

We resumed.

Then stopped.

"Why?" she asked.

"It's important," I said.

She thought about this for a bit.

"You and I are not alone." She said.

"I appreciate it," said I.

Victorian hugged me. She set her jacket, firmly pressed against my chest. I placed my hands around her tight waistline. And I felt her good warmth, and also slightly more complete, again.

"Does it ever feel like time is going by faster, this decade?" she asked.

"Sometimes," I answered. Sometimes I notice.

Quite often, Lady Vi reassured me. She clung to me tightly.

We went to an party that night. She felt this would pick me up.

At the Big Live state party.

Re-translated and modernized:

Leanne: "Why don't you get along with her these days?"

"We don't. There was an incident, way back when, and just a few years ago too."

"Did you speak to her about it?"

No.

Carole: "Whatever, she's like forty."

I started to laugh.

"Hon, if Hanna's like forty, then I'm like, twenty."

"But she, is, like forty."

"Hon, Hanna is well over six hundred years old."

"That sounds like nonsense. Sometimes you talk nonsense, Herkomar."

"It's not nonsense. She's over <u>six hundred</u> years old. We're <u>immortals</u>. That's how I met her."

Carole: "Do you want to hug me again?"

"Sure."

So I hugged Carole. Then I hugged Leanne. Then I was brought to attention two more very good-looking excellent blonde female lawyers after that.

After a thought: "So what was the incident?"

"She killed someone," I said.

"How?"

"She struck someone in the eye."

There was a whole race of them, I mentioned to her.

"Oh," is what Carole said. Leanne nodded.

Carole: "You mean like Pay-guns?"

"Not really."

"Like in Mythology." mentioned another woman.

"Not really." A pause. "Or, sort of, actually. They were more like giants. Sort of, actually, very," I thought.

"Wow." She said.

End of chapter.

At this point, I feel it worth addressing some complaints, by very modern users, that my book, and up to this point, as well, is somewhat very, very highly male chauvinistic. For this, I see thanks to defend, a bit, since this is what the times were actually like, historically, to my memory.

To say, I often write explicitly about conquests with good-looking women, because, this of course, was, about what my life and I, Herkomar, actually, and very, very accurately, dealt with, for most of the time, during those middle periods.

Also, please note, 'male' chauvinism did not seem entirely that bad, back in the fourteenth through the eighteenth century, and the eighteenth through the twenty-first century, and much, much later. Quite often good-looking women found this trait very, very endearing on a man of my type, back when.

I'll also include,
Primarily, and historically, very good-looking women were often seen as important. Which I defend, because we were a race of artists and good artisans, and aesthetics were quite often highly important and prized by good-looking males.

Thank you.

Chauvinism forever, right?

-Herkomar

5

THE 1550S

the story of levay, and alexia

What made the 1550s truly special, for us, is, that this was the decade that I was first introduced to levay. This is a story I don't tell very often, and this is a story that I don't like telling either. After the initial meetings with him, we found out that Levay was, in fact, a total numf--ker, a deft scoundrel, and a totally horr*b** piece of trash, as well.

The story of Levay, and his final undoing, is, also, in fact, actually a very important story, in our personal history sometimes.

Immortals are highly sensitive beings.

We are seemingly fragile quite often.

-Herkomar

The Trinity

One of our couriers passed me the note. It had been dated, 1556:

Important discovery, it read.

Communicae opened with man from 1438.

Over a hundred eighteen years old!.
Remembers events quite clearly.
With, reputation of Knowledge.
Would like to meet you.
Heard word of Herkomar.
Please send back response, if interested.
Thank you.

Initially:
Curious, my interest, was piqued. And, Overjoyed, in fact, was this news for me. A new immortal had been discovered, it indicated to me.

The item ran from close to Paris, the country of Rouen. Craikendorff Castle, it read on the cover of the note. Item 39. Along the Road.

The name written was: LeVay.

My response, which I wrote:
Simply extraordinary.
I, Herkomar, the Best,
would be most pleased, of course, to open a new channel, for such an interesting enthralling individual.
If pleased yourself, please send meeting card.
We operate from Venice. And areas of London. Thank you.

I sent back my response. Via quick service.

It took them a week for them to get to me:

Welcomme;
My name is; LeVay
Meet me, and (^my) sister, at Castle Craikendorff.
I own large multiplex.
Drop by for an appointment. In November.

Present card, at the gate. For
Two weeks stay in Paris,
at my good address.
Should be written on the back of card.
Good time.
Thank you.
Love Honey.
-LeVay

Outstanding, I thought. This could be the start of a new adventure for me and the rest of us. Thrilled, I mentioned this to Hanna, and also, to Constiglione.

Hanna acted somewhat abrasive about the article. She simply didn't have time for that nonsense. Constiglione seemed somewhat indifferent, and, however, still, he was very supportive.

Apparently, I was the only one truly excited about the new discovery.

November was at least eight months away. But perhaps I would pay visit to the man and his castle for an earlier drop by, or perhaps invite the man over to one of our totally fine estates held in Venice or upper London.

I sent over another reply:

How would you like a happy stay in Venice.
We would be happy to entertain, in our great centers.
Let me know.
-Herkomar

I waited three weeks for a response. And then it came.

It read plainly,

No.
You didn't read letter.
We don't leave country!
You come by here.
Paris!!!!
Or I rescind.
-LeVay

Um, okay, this sounded fine. Clearly I would not test him. Immortals, were, by my figuring, highly important to the world.

Did you ever find out if he was an immortal?, a woman asked me at one point.

Yes, I found out later, when I visited him, that he, LeVay, could lay claim that he was indeed an immortal, as well.

That was beside the point, Hanna later reminded me.

I made an appointment to speak with LeVay in August. We rode partially by stagecoach, me with a female model named Clarissa, and also, the good Lady I. Victorian, accompanying us as well.

Paris was a central city. We had made several stops along the way, for good purchase of good wines. I myself was known not to indulge in wine or liquors, however, we were often collecting the good vintage years for purposes or high return salability. Generally '32 was always one of the more sellable.

Also, cheese was, back then, a high luxury product, signifying a good degree of high opulence, which we would bring, along with the dark wine and other products, to LeVay, as gifts for his household.

Not astonishing, was that he also lived in a castle. Immortals are quite often known to collect very large degrees of wealth. Lady Victorian, as well, had deed possessions of at least one or two strong large micro buildings, of her own, in areas around upper London and England and Venice. I myself once inherited a large private estate fourteenth century style castle, back in the early years, in Germany, but however, after certain migratory conditions broke loose during a certain autumn period, I was forced to abandon it.

I was, at that point, in 1322, wanted by the law slightly, over a misunderstanding concerning the quick sale transaction of some large grey lightly broken weeding and farming instruments, which I, in fact, had some moderately light involvement in. I was surely not the same as I am nowadays. One of my neighbors claimed he had been bilked. That had not been my serious intention.

I remember that story for a reason, quite often.

Upon our arrival at Craikendorff Castle,

We arrived in the evening, and were slightly welcomed by a small group of servants. We waited in the front garden room, together. I. Victorian milled a bit. She pulled out a rolled cigarette, and smoked it in the open.

Clarissa put her hand over my leg. We had been sitting patiently.

One of the servants brought out a light bread snack with cottage cream, over it.

He explained.

Their master Lord, to whom they referred to as LeVay, was busy in the study, and would be out, with his sister, Alexia, to host, for us shortly.

"HaHA!", he, LeVay, proclaimed, upon our first introduction. He carried about a knight sword.

LeVay, to us, looked around twenty-six or twenty-seven years of age. He seemed partially amicable and also somewhat good-looking. His light brown hair, swept upwards, and clearly held some sort of product to maintain its intended coarseness and lift.

His sister seemed slightly younger-looking by about a year or two. She wore her very blonde hair nicely. Actually, I found her to be quite pretty.

"The master has not been expecting you today," he said loudly.

Victorian was lightly amused by this. What a dummy, must've thought Clarissa.

"Don't worry about it," he said. "I'll show you three to the guest quarters. For your stay, m'lady."

Our guest quarters were more than adequate. The large white and red roominess, with very good partitioning, was supplemented well. Paintings of pure light gold, were held on the walls, well.

The next morning we had breakfast with our hosts, and discussed, of course, the nature of our being. Alexia had been alive for at least one hundred and fourteen years. LeVay had been at least four years older, at the time.

They both didn't age, and looked in their mid-twenties, as mentioned.

One thing, I'll comment, Alexia happened to be surprisingly mean to me. On a conversation regarding,

She called me a dope and a dill-linger.

She hit me with a rough apple at, at least eight points.

I became slightly angered.

In discussions I'd make open rant against her, sort of. Surely she was pretty, but I didn't have the time. I was purely more experienced.

In conversations, I'd side with LeVay completely. I considered him a friend.

"What the f' is wrong with her?" I'd ask, referring to his sister.

LeVay merely shrugged. I quite liked spending time with him sometimes, I thought.

"Why do you put up with her nonsense?" I asked again.

"She's just somebody," he tried to explain.

Maybe, I thought to myself. Clarissa agreed, and she held tightly to my arms. Worried a bit, she seemed. And, So I cared deeply for her, Clarissa, I meant.

In the meantime, Lady Victoria busied herself with some of the upper horsemen with gigantic muscles who were staying there in some of the guest cottages. There actually happened to be more than one guest cottage. A bunch of these muscle guys set up residence in these minor chalets. The theory was, they were guest friends of Alexia. Victorian spent her time, talking with these men, and charming them.

On the third night, Alexia came in my room, that night, and huggeded me.

I held her close, and embraced her long across her shoulders and arms.

On the fourth night, the next day, LeVay kicked us out of his castle.

Sorry, I said, but this seemed to mean not much to him.
"Get out of my Castle right now," he said firmly.

And so, we left, leaving our gifts behind, and I softly vowed to myself that I'd one day later redeem myself, and hopefully mend the situation with my fellow immortal custodians, LeVay and his darling blonde younger sister, Alexia.

Eight months went by. Two years went by.
I felt bad about the ordeal, with LeVay. Had it been my fault?

My thought was that I should've been more respectful to him.

I sent over an antique brilliant mirror. Gold-plated, and very expensive-looking. I had bought it for a fair price at the market, with the price tag, of 2000 currency, which I left attached on the gift, for his record.

He sent it back to me, slightly broken. With a dent, and a crack in it.

The message, LeVay's, read:

Sorry,
But this broken mirror that you sent, is broken.
It is no longer usable, by me.
Please send more.

This made me feel pretty bad, in fact. I hadn't intended the gift I sent him to be impolite. Possibly I would have the mirror repaired, and re-sent over. Which I did. Plus, an apology note maybe, as well, I considered writing one.

Next, I decided to send over a pair of guest servants.

A male was selected, a young male by the name of Friesse. Friesse's mother, had sent her son to work for me, in hopes that he would find a better life and a good worker occupation. I always figured some work would be good for the lad.

Also, a young blonde-haired femme, named Eleanor, was picked for choice. She was working at the time, for Constiglione, as an artist's model. There was not much she wouldn't do for me. Eleanor was in love with me, and she would gladly serve LeVay if I requested of her.

I sent the two of them over to act as servants for LeVay, if he would accept them as servants, if he desired. They were a nice-looking duo, and I was fairly certain that LeVay would most likely accept.

This, to me, would mend things.

Later I found out what he had done. He had done something _wrong_!

It came in a box. With the message:

Thank you for your kindly gift.
These are all that is left of them.
For I have keelt them. De-d.
-LeVay

I'm actually very amazed that LeVay had the g-ts. to actually sign the note.

Contained in the box was a slightly wet lock of long blonde servants hair.

This situation scared and even slightly traumatized me, quite a bit.

My eyes went wet. I did not hold back. I was so distraught, and totally frantic.

If I had mentioned anything about the situation to Constiglione, I knew he'd start screaming about it. As mentioned, Eleanor was one of his prized art models. I had even loved Eleanor at some point. I wanted to mention this to Constiglione, but I never found the opportunity.

And, if I mentioned the situation about it, to Friessc's mother, she'd be totally heart-broken. I didn't have the courage to tell her that someone that I had sent her son to work as a servant for, had done something so absolutely terrible.

Instead, I reasoned I'd go to Hanna about it, and I told her the whole story.

Man, was she infuriated. She started hurling books all over the place. She hit me over the head with a hard copy of Jacques Turner's non-famous written memoirs.

How could you be so irresponsible! she screamed at me.

She was only slightly angry with me, but she was totally, totally, enraged about LeVay.

She had decided that we, she and I, would go to LeVay's Castle, and that was where she would be determined to murder him with her bare hands, if necessary, she said. If he had indeed hurt one of our servants, she included.

She took a good pair of war gloves, a long sharp knife and a large battle sword with her. I actually knew she could do something like this. I've seen her do this before, on at least two separate occasions.

I was slightly worried, again. Hanna might call for me to fight. I had not seriously fought with another immortal in at least eight or nine years.

The ride over to Castle Craikendorff seemed fairly long and uneventful.

"Just don't talk to me right now," said Hanna. On our way over she had been very rude to me.

"Sorry... sorry. Fine," I muttered apologetically.

When we reached Craikendorff, we discovered two things.

First off, we, Hanna and I, didn't have to deal with the issue of murdering LeVay. He had gone crazy, is what one of the other servants, at the Castle, had reported to me. After a week and a half of his madness, LeVay had apparently killed himself, by drinking a jar of poisonous mud drink. They buried him in the backyard, in a plot, the servants said.

We asked them, had LeVay murdered any of the servants

recently. They acted as if that was not totally out of the ordinary. That actually seemed pretty scary to me. I thought so, anyway.

Secondly, Alexia was no longer living there. She had moved away, purportedly, shortly after our initial stay, at least a year and a half ago. They distributed a card to me, of apparently a hotel area that she might've been staying in. For a point, I thought I'd track her down.

Maybe not, suggested Hanna. Hanna seemed vaguely satisfied, I guess.

They say that God cries, when an immortal dies.
I sure hoped so. I sure hoped so.

6

THE 1570S

purported rumor that Hanna has killed Alexia

At least eight years after the incident with LeVay, his sister came to visit me in Venice.

I was packing up at the grove stand, when I saw her. She still looked very pretty. Her blonde hair was set nicely.

"Herkomar?"

"How'd you find me?" I asked her.

Alexia thought for a quick moment. "I waited at the carriage station for you."

"Mmm. I couldn't make it. Too busy, I guess," I responded.

"You actually care about me, Herkomar, I thought...."

"I do,"

"they sent me your card. And I wanted to drop by."

"hon, I want you to live," I told her.

I then gave her a hug. It seemed somewhat non-appropriate.

Afterwards, I charmed her with a little small talk.

"You're so good at talking to women, Herkomar," she said to me.

And two years after that.
We had another encounter.

"You are wearing a very nice dress," I told her.
"I like the way you walk," she, Alexia, said to me, politely.
"Thank you," I mentioned. I gave her a very long tight smile.

Yes, it was a very pleasant day indeed, she nodded. Between the two of us, truly glorious. She had incredible blue eyes, as well.
And then, we served out for a large brunch.

Hanna later scolded me about the private meeting with alexia. She, Hanna, had only known of one of these meetings, I speculated.
I loved alexia though, and I only wanted for her to be happy.
After the incident with her brother, I felt I had to protect her, somewhat.

Don't meet with her again, Hanna told me.
You have total roomfuls of good-looking women with which to spend time, Herkomar. If you meet with Alexia again, however, I may be forced to punish her, very very severely, she said.
I didn't bother asking why.
Hanna's mind was clearly set about it. To Hanna; Alexia and LeVay were basically the same thing. They were connected by blood, and they even had the same name: LeVay.

If Alexia returned to Venice again, Hanna would gladly have her destroyed. Hanna said this seriously.

She felt I had caused too many problems with this situation. It's surely not right anyway, she figured.

Hanna had killed at least three of my good friends, or, three or four unknown fellows, since I'd known her. Plus, according to history, she had also killed off that other mystery race of earlier immortals, the Circuits. "of Nine", of whichever, I remembered her mentioning a slight few times. That, also she wrote about that briefly in the intro to this book.

A few years later, and Alexia was gone.

I tried to contact her several times, but she was missing at her address. Reportedly a small hotel, just outside eastern Europe.

She was still missing, where I looked. I sent a note to Craikendorff, and they said they'd send me additional info, if any ever came, but none ever did, and they didn't respond back after a while, for at least after two or three weeks at a time.

Not great, about the situation.
I wondered what to do about it.

"Did you vanish my friend, Hanna?" I asked Hanna.
"No, Herkomar, I did not vanish Alexia," she said to me. Coldly. She looked as if she wanted to stab me when she said that.

Fine.

There were rumors that she had Alexia vanished anyway. I did not debunk these rumors.

I presented my heart to Hanna, and she punched me lightly in the dong. I was semi-sleeping at the time. I knew she could punch way harder, but she didn't.

What a coward sometimes, I thought of her, but I would not say this out loud.

Unexpected, this actually strengthened my relationship with Hanna.

After a bit, I decided to let it rest.

She, Hanna, also sent me a book, two or four years later, as a present, which I may talk about later, in another chapter, or in this chapter, in fact. To help you write your book, she told me.

It's sort of interesting. I had no idea about Hanna, that she was so intellectually gifted and attractive. I mean, I thought she was attractive for her age. She looked around sixty or forty-five quite often, but, even so, she had a likeable cute and very pretty and very smart-looking appeal. Some sort of effect, even on younger guys.

"Thank you, Herkomar." –says Hanna

A few more words about the book that Hanna had sent me. It seemed often part history book, and also, quite often, part science book. Supposedly, the book was written by a friend of hers. Several sections were enlightening. Some actually, very incredible. There were some sections on how to build wings if needed. A weapon section was also included, on how to use military items, and different techniques.

And, also, I found that one unique section, that I was definitely going to include in a chapter, in my book. Heh, heh, heh. I had found the section, for which I was looking, that discusses the period that would be referred to as, and known as, the early, early Darker Ages. Also, the book included a disclaimer, that book language was toned down a bit, for private use of friends, with backgrounds as historians, of course.

One content, of slight major:
The Fourteen H-Razors, The Circuits. of Nine, they were called. I mean, we all want to know who the previous immortals were, among Hanna's generation, right? Good Grak!, they were hor**b*e cr*d. I feel so totally totally superior to them after reading about what hor**b*e, t*rrible, ev*l pieces of cr*d they were.

Listed are the figures, on the list, and several hor**fic terrible acts that they had c*mmitted, and how they were later, in fact, in their last and final years, snuffed out from existence, for their crim*inal actions. Basically, all of the H-Razors are already always deceased, except for hanna. There had been fourteen of them, which I've copied. I'm fairly certain that Hanna's friend would've said it was okay for me to do so. Thank you.

This, I present to you, in these notes, loosely adapted from the book that Hanna presented to me:

Disclaimer: Acts of murder, and acts of rape and hurtful damage to others, especially innocent individuals, are always wrong; and are not condoned by the author of this work, ever.

1.   Takkus-not sure

2. Krill, Master of Evil-deceased, assassinated, set on fire, by whom, was unknown.
3. Bay?, Bayr Mayer ??? or something like that. not sure, don't know who this is, someone mentioned this individual is probably not around anymore anyway, can put this aside. His whereabouts unknown
4. E'Se'rajel the Cruel-drank human blood, which was pre-pared, bathed in the blood of other women, killed a hostage once by crushing his head off. She was deceased, killed by Hanna.
5. Orleof the Sly- executed over 40 men; sla*ghtered over 28 hostages, t*rtured them first, and put their heads on spics afterwards. He had been deceased, killed by Hanna.
6. Xerxes IX-cut anelder hostage's hands once, then forced them to eat poop for ten years. Xerxes had been deceased, stabbed by Hanna.
7. Axe Masher-used to ch*p, the heads of several individuals, with a war axe, sometimes, and several persons body, with a war axe, sometimes. He had been also deceased, killed by Hanna.
8. Polpe Mekueletto-r*ped women, at least 8 of them, fed pr*s'ners to animals, known for setting male hostages on fl*m. He had been deceased, killed, and set on fire.
9. Krill III, of no relation.-had a man physically t*rtured, in public arena, a large stadium. p*lled men apart, with chari-ots, also, he horribly disf*gured a young women at least once. Krill III had been deceased, murdered, assassinated, and set on fire.
10. L. Croaley the Wizener, who had killed a merchant, who stole money from him. He had been deceased, or assassinated.
11. O'Terrey, the Drifter-once claimed he had three wives. He had _three_ wives! she let him live, told him to get the f' out of town, before she _really_ became angry,
12. Lyn*tte the Stranger-po*red a vial of homemade ac*d

solution on a rival competitor's head. She had been de-ceased, or assassinated by Hanna.

13. Hannah, the Brave One-spirit like, eem., Hanna, her. Yes, she says, she had been on the listing once! That was why I _knew_ to have basically all of them destroyed. All evil must die!!!, she says.

14. Ant??? Ant??? Ant, Ant, something or other. unsure, can't figure out, maybe, leave alone-probably he eats mice. Who knows? Was he deceased, as well?; His whereabouts had been listed as unknown

Hanna de-reassured me that every single one on the list, was an actual real life being from the eighth to tenth century.

Her stories, she explained, were actually surprisingly, all checkable.

Also,

"Be careful, now, son, some of these guys might've had heirs," she said. "And some of those heirs might be fairly angry with me these days for canceling, attending action on, their parents, huh?" she said.

"Yes, I guess....," I said. Why did Hanna have to make me feel like a young sometimes?, I wondered.

"Although, quite possibly..., probably not though." She added.

I agreed.

"Who was Number one?" I asked.

Who knows? She said. Legends, and also certain prestigious ru-mors maybe; was her best answer.

"And Number two?"

Probably not alive anymore. The top three, she explained were apparently the leadership command. Equivalent to comptrollers, she explained.

Also, Number three, himself, apparently had not been authentically sighted by anyone of who she knew.

And number four.

Hanna explained that she managed to eliminate number four, and, additionally, about eight more of them, in a very large minor sweep.

"A minor sweep?"

That's roughly equivalent to a week and five days. A long major sweep seemed equivalent to slightly more than approximately two and a half months.

That's right, she said.

She had to eliminate a bunch of them, in a very quick amount of time.

The more planning there was, sometimes the harder it would be, she explained.

Number five had been a traveling warlord, of some sort.

Number six had been a renegade colonel, it turned out. The notation explained that Hanna stabbed them, which I now realize is probably also totally true. I skipped through the rest of them.

The brief list continued.

"Number 11?"

That was O'Terrey. Hanna told me that she had to let O'Terrey live, he just wasn't as harmful as the other ones. And Hanna figured he might be useful at some point, in the situation that she needed someone to collaborate.

"Don't worry," she said. "He won't bother us. He was given a very severe warning. He'll probably never pay visit here ever, most likely."

Also I asked Hanna later, who number 14 was.
"I found that out later." she said. "His real name was, Antonelle,"
"Antonelle?"
"Yes," she said. "His name was, Antonelle LeVeii."

"Pretty good, Hanna." I had been very impressed, in fact.

She suggested I add more to this chapter, but later.

7

THE 1580S

Hanna does a demonstration on keys

More information, when I looked up in the book that Hanna had procured for me. (date. 1579)

In the book that she bought me, Hanna is actually mentioned quite a bit. Her name appears in at least four very important chapters, as a very important individual as well. Quite naturally, as I said, I was impressed by this.

Also, the book itself:

It spends at least eleven chapters discussing the opium poppy.

Also, discussed, with certain mixtures of the coke plant, new age drinking agents could be formulated. Cola was later established two, or two and a half, centuries later.

I pondered concocting a few mixtures, per instructions, at some point.

"Has Constiglione seen this book?"

"Not yet," she answered. Probably she wasn't going to get him a copy at all, I bet.

Books were hard to find, quite often.

Also, moreover, according to the book that Hanna obtained for me, cigarettes had yet to be formulated in several areas, the book had intended. Opium, however, was quite often found not regulated.

Yet, in fact: Use of opium had proved beneficial to one's intellect, for a variety of chemical reasons, and others.

One, opium, as well, is known for chemical properties that regulate blood flow and circulation, quite often, This was definitely approved as correct.

Two, that smoke from opium itself contains high quantities of wind element; wind can often be conceived as a high business speed variable. I was not sure about this, or if this was actually correct. Why did they include this in the book? I wondered, and, also, fire element; assuredly, proper usage of opium is often integral to human warmth, personal warmth, and elements of total unconditional love, which can be found within the opium seed, truly opium is a blessing.

Three, due to satisfaction of, and connection with, certain genius mystic societies, great world knowledge is absorbed with each inhalation from a good roll. This, I actually was pretty sure, was very correct. also, very apparent from this, ingestion of opium will probably definitely increase good looks, or, to enhance, they meant, I guessed, and greatly increase very, very high sophistication, and incredible prowess, of course.

Four, the usage of opium demonstrates power of man. We are in the battle to survive.

Also...

Five, with mourning, wisdom is granted. This article seemed somewhat innate, however integral.

Six, the brain and intelligence increases, for many, many reasons also due to regard of smoker's plane. This was very, very good, was the comment.

"Smoker's plane?" I asked.

Seven, the book explained, that objects in closer dimension contributed to increased speed quotient and movement level. This was important.

Eight, high level consumption of opium adds quick dimensions that increase speed, increase intelligence, and, therefore, often increases motion sense which is often highly connected to high speed and brain power. A lot of this information I had already known before, however, I was quite pleased that someone had written on this info.

Ingestion of opium causes relief from pain. (ater, I knew, opium would be used in heroin.

"It helps win marathons," suggested Hanna.
"That's right," I said.
"Also, it deals with the moon, and, most particularly, the sun," she also added.
"I gotcha, baby," I said to her.

And, Also,

Nine, Opium increased communication skills, and smart prowess ability, and additionally, increased personal fluidity and increased athletic fluidity of toned athletic bodies, is, are all, highly, highly tested results. These results could not be defeated, the book assured.; also, another item, leaf rolls are often highly connected with nature. I wondered how Hanna felt about this citation.

for which, I also add, too:

Ten, basically, no one dies unless they want to die. I was fairly certain, that this was a medical fact.

For a time, I waited.

Next:

Another book demo on color coding, was also a slightly worthwhile one, and also mildly very amusing.

A good-looking colored nationalist friend of mine, later took issue with this section chapter. As I explained, the intentions of the book were assumingly innocuous. For my own duty record, I happen to defend many individuals of all religions, and several distinct light blue color nations, as well, quite often. As mentioned, this, was not my intent, to portray such needless allegory. However, that being explained, this is as the other book read....

The Book demo explained:

The gold key, it explained, represented a token of luck and love. Also, magic, involving luxury items, and money items, or florins.

The red key, represented a symbol of fire, and there, also represented a symbol of love. Also, the red key represented power and strength, and good esteem. Courage and valor, as well, it reminded me often.

The blue key, represented wind and water, and therefore, related to human physiology, and also high intellect and influence, and wisdom, as well, I had once remembered.

White, of course represented protection and divinity, and magic of great, and healing, and light magic.

Yellow represented transportation and movement of travel, and light and spirit.

Importantly, the Violet key, in belief, represented patronage, but, however, most often, was associated with great divinity, and served as a neutral form of white coding. Also, moreover, the violet key provided as a fusion color, key, of blue, and also, red.

Of these colors, there were probably only four color keys that were really generally used, which were listed: Red, blue, gold, and white. In this theory, the book postulated, those four main colors always, always outranked all other colors. Red magic in particular, was known to succeed, at a very high rate.

And, also, furthermore, Two other colors were thought to be important, and in situations, to be highly recognized. The color grey represented metals, and transformation of metal stock, and change and alteration, as mentioned there. Black often represented bold distinction, and chaos and darkness, but also formality.

Each key had a complementary, and oppositional color. Black often opposed white. Silver often complemented gold. Pink supplemented blue. And so on, and so forth.

This was all very important, the other book read.

And, then, after that, Hanna said to me, "These are all yours.", and she handed me a copy of the yellow ones.
Keys represent good luck, quite often, she mentioned.

"Pretend they represent money," she said.
And I thanked her. And she gave me a hug, and some additional instructions. I was to embark.

I reminded myself that Hanna was considered very incredibly pretty back when.
Nowadays then, by the 1580s, she was also considered heartachingly cute.

"Thank you."

Part I, section i.

And then we went off on our intrepid voyage, dated 1581.

"What do you got there, man?" a crewman asked me.

"They're a set of yellow keys. They represent good fortune, I guess. From Hanna."

"Do you actually buy her nonsense?"

"Her nonsense, by the way, happens to be, all true. I happen to know."

"What?" He paused.

He suddenly froze, a bit, and then he seemed somewhat embarrassed.

"Yeah....She wanted me to check on some stuff for her," I said, "I guess, while she's away."

He seemed sort of very, very nervous. About something, I guess.

"So, yeah," I said again. "Are you okay?" I asked him.

"Excuse me, I have to get to another spot for a moment," he said. And he walked off.

Whatever. I thought to myself a moment.

Our trip to England remained vaguely uneventful.

The 1580s. Section II

Upon arrival, we settled.

I had purchased us a good flat in upper London, a few months previous. Lady Victorian, myself, and Constiglione.

We drank from bottles of expensive water, for that time.

We had been kicked out of Italy, once again.

The incident was a minor incident, yet even after all those years, enough became enough.

There had been another scandal in Lady Victorian's market, which had at that point, been renamed, Bunny's Place Market.

There had been a dispute over some high class purchase; and seeing that the man involved with the dispute, was highly good-looking and very masculine, one of the very good-looking femmes that counciled in the area, offered to settle the dispute, as very, very good-looking women often were known to do, by offering a kiss on him. Which she did, as I was told, of the incident, in one of the open spaces of the free market area.

So the decision had been made. We would have to close operations for a period of at least two months, given the scandal, and several other previous minor incidents.

Our own decision had been made too. It was time for a vacation, to which we'd re-open our offices again. One of the options happened to be Berlin. However, at the time, we ultimately decided on England, for reasons dealing with a large deal purchase.

We'd remain there for an indeterminate amount of time; which at this point, probably meant at least two or fourteen years in London, at least.

We stayed on the high third floor of the building, that I'd purchased.

I poured a cup of water for the both of them. Constiglione drank from the bottle.

He sat on a wood box.

"So what's new with the business sector, right now?" I said. I was joking, somewhat.

Lady Victorian smoked a cigarette, then drank from her water. She picked up a book from the shelf, and began reciting from French. The book's title: The Heavenly doves of London. By J.J. Garette.

"But If I were to become, Then That so lives it..." she read, on and on.

"That's very good," I said. "Amuse us, Vi."

I started cracking up. Constiglione looked sort of tired.

Then we took a break.

8

THE 1590S

discovery of lightermann

Ten years later.

There was an incident in Sweden. Someone new apparently had been discovered, as of year date 1593.

"Vandergaard?" I asked.

"That's his name," someone pointed out.

When we initially found Vandergaard, he had been wandering the streets. He had been wandering the streets of Sweden for over six decades. I personally dealt with the investigation. They brought me in as an expert.

"Vandergaard?"

"Pickup ze beau... , coop?" he said to me. He wore darkened clothes, and a large blue wrap. He was speaking some form of Swedish. A woman served him a bowl of warm stew.

"How old is he?" I asked.

"He's been cited as being around sixty-eight years of age, or maybe older," said the man sent from the fillgates commission. He, Vandergaard, was able to recall and describe very early events better than expected, and very accurately.

"His birthday predates the rest of ours," someone else explained.

Interesting, I thought. Also, I thought that comment was actually very slightly rude. But whatever.

I looked over the notes.

Reports: Some actually remembered him from over four decades ago, they said.

"We questioned...highly...," said one of them.

We did some quick testing.

Now, he, lightermann, or vandergaard; had the appearance of a very good-looking young man, about sixteen years of age. He seemed very highly intelligent. This had also been determined, through the testing. Also, women probably found him to be very, very good-looking.

"He's definitely one of yours, right?" said the man from fillgates. "He's clearly one of your kind, I mean," he corrected himself.

"He's definitely someone, that our type of Order might definitely find interesting," I answered, in Swedish. "I myself don't travel much to Sweden." I admitted.

"Does he have relatives? A family?"

"We did a look up of him," the man from fillgates answered. "His actual parents expired over sixty years ago..."

"His actual parents expired at least over sixty years ago,

according to the dock," someone said. "Vandergaard was all they had."

"Still. His issue." "Unknown, mystery figure, huh?"

I examined his eyes lightly.

"He doesn't age." Someone else, a female, pointed out.

"That's clearly one of yours, right?"

"We'll take him in," I said, and nodded.

"Trachten ze vall et., dooushe," said lightermann.

Also, another include, I'd like to send thanks to the good men and very excellent women of the fillgates commission, for making this chapter possible. You guys rock.

We agreed to terms of settlement for Lightermann. I left about sixty or eighty thousand at the desk. Then arranged for transport, for him, to England.

I said I'd explain later why we sometimes referred to vandergaard as lightermann. But, Perhaps I'll mention why later, in another chapter. It's actually sort of a cute story, as to why we had his name changed.

Lightermann could only speak three languages, we found out later. He knew vague native Swedish, some German, and just a bit of English. (I myself speak at least over twenty or twenty-five different languages. Victorian knew at least three or four.)

New English was no bore to him. He managed to learn somewhat over the next few years. And one of ours taught him how to read, very well.

Training lightermann to interact with civilized society turned out to be no serious chore. Women found him to be strikingly good-looking and absolutely charming.

Also, grooming him was not difficult. He seemed to look at least fairly decent, most times. We purchased a higher separate flat in London, for which he could stay.

He took care of himself after that.

Lunch with Janice:

"So what's on the horizons for next year?" she asked me.
"Probably," I said.
I was thinking about going to Spain for a year or too, and then leaving aside some major work until then.
"What's to deal in Spain?"
"Who knows," I brought up.
She gave me a light hug, and someone whistled.

More to this chapter, on this decade:

Another event: There was a female prophet named O. Wanda. O. Wanda herself, in that decade, had formulated a new code for writing.

I looked over her specs.

Her work seemed, to me, rather entirely very brilliant. The new code she developed, pertained to a modified alphabet listing, with at least thirty-seven highly superior derived alphabet symbols. Each of her letter symbols represented a practical position, and also, a political platform. There were also some very good notes of highly careful construction. Incidentally, her alphabet held at least eight different versions of the modern swastika.

Very Brilliant, it seemed to me, I said.

Also: Another flyer.

An artist named Davide had invented a new flying machine.

Actual flying machines would be later invented in the Americas, close to the end of the nineteenth century.

Apparently, Davide's machine could roll somewhere slightly above twenty feet. Lately it merely rolled along, at good presentation, and he was pelted with dry vegetables, after that. It actually flew very well, I heard at some point later.

I myself handed him a good two hundred for his work. I considered his, a serious and noble effort. Piloted flying machines were invented later, to my knowledge.

Now, the reason I mention him is, coincidentally,

Two years later, Davide was commissioned to paint a highly valuable, highly prized portrait of Lady Victorian, complete with her white blouse, and well fashioned skirt.

Davide was, after all that, considered a great and celebrated artist, and a genius.

The Renaissance will never be over, man!

PART II

The Modern Period
(late Renaissance)

1610s-constiglione goes to arabia
1620s-story about China, India
1630s-meeting with Richelieu
1650s-lightermann attends new world conference
1670s-article on muskets, age of piracy, visit to Spain, England
The late 1680s-colonialism, currency, they settle on America
1690s-argument over printing press, introduction of spade

9

THE 1610S

constiglione goes to Arabia

After that, Constiglione was required for work in Arabia for a period of time. Two and a half years, actually, he spent there.

Apparently, he was conducting a field study. Someone else had written a book.

The book, in expertise, was a collection of six stories, written by a very high range British scholar. Tales of the Arabian Nights had been published, and collected, close to a century later. Constiglione was sent to investigate.

The street markets were actually generally abided excellence. Someone had employed a high order function to prevent thievery mishaps.

He stayed in the backroom of a restaurant dine center, which he had paid for use, as temporary shelter. Someone had given him the name of the restaurant. He had abided.

"What do you know about Arabian myth and folklore?" he asked someone, in the market, which he later mentioned to me.

Apparently, they knew much.

Four original tales, collected by Constiglione on his visit to Iran!!!! per my later translation, to modernized English.

Story One: A wand orchestra is in town for a series. The first night, the wand conductor is not feeling well, so a moderately trained cellist is brought in to conduct the wand orchestra, at which he does very well. This happens again, on the second night, and the string cellist conducts, once again, absolutely perfectly. Now, on the third night, the wand conductor feels a little better, so they thank the cellist, and send him back to his section.

The woman next to him says, 'Hey, where have you been for the past few days?"

Story Two: A man buys a box, which he takes home, back with him. Inside contains the body of a young lady. She emerges from the box to give the guy a warm hug and serve him a tea beverage, careful to please him. Then she gets back in the box and falls asleep, like a good little young lady.

Story Three: A new world colonist is having dinner with an Arabian friend of his, and he starts bragging about his ingenue with business women. The Arabian is interested. He owns a private club, and he puts his friend to a challenge, to see who can intrigue more women. The new world colonist manages to intrigue at least three good-looking finance women in one night, and puts three straight line markings on a table board, to signify three satisfactory business treaties. The next morning, they meet up, and the Arabic friend confesses that the new world colonist has beaten his score by two. "By two?" asks the new world colonist. "Yes," his friend admits. "I could only manage one hundred and nine."

Story Four: A young man is involved with a plot to murder his uncle, over and including the caliph's throne. He later assaults the father of his girlfriend, accidentally, and beats up on her brother way bad. Over the misunderstanding, the whole audience kills themselves.

"Sounds like good intrigue," says Constiglione. "I'll take this one."

He purchases a gold metal lamp. which later he brings back to share with us.

"I purchased this metal lamp at a market." he says to us. "I'll let you know how it works."

"I know something else that grants wishes," mentions, Vi.
"That's gorgeous, that's just gorgeous," I said.
"One moment, Vi, I'm trying to think here...." says Constiglione.
We love you, Vi, totally.

We love you, Vi. Totally. There's a pause.

Constiglione continues, "So, anyway... you rub on the magic

metal lamp, and if you rub on it three times, then apparently it grants wishes."

"Really? Sounds grand," I admitted. I picked up the metal lamp. "Here let me try it. Let see how it works."

"Now give me some space." I said.

I rubbed the lamp.

"One," I said. Lady V. started cracking up.

I rubbed the lamp again.

"Two," I said.

I waited a moment in order to build a little suspense.

And then I rubbed the lamp, a third time.

"There," I said.

And then the three of us, including Lady V., and Constiglione, were surrounded by a huge ball of blue-white light.

Later...

"Was that it?" I asked.

"I guess," said Constiglione.

"What happened?"

"Did our wishes come true?" asked Vi.

"Maybe." Constiglione scratched his head a bit. He took the lamp back away. "We should put this away for now," he suggested.

Lady V. frowned.

I realize that this next anecdote comes across as a repetition of story number two, but actually it's very slightly different.

A funny thing happened, after that, about two days or a week after.

I was visited by a guest, a very good-looking blonde woman, in a cute white blouse and a very cute black skirt.

She came into my visiting quarters, pushed me on an open seat, and gave me one of the better excellent higher quality warm kisses I've ever received

"Thank you, Master," she said to me.

She then dropped a handful of cards on the counter. And then she left.

Constiglione, of course, had employed several many good-looking young women, however, he very rarely mismanaged them ever, as such.

Nowadays I'm actually convinced the blonde woman was sent by Lady V.

I asked V. about this later, in fact, and she sort of agreed.

She sort of vaguely knew what I was talking about. Also she vaguely remembered sending a young blonde woman at some point, to someone.

And more, I guess:

The name of the young blonde woman who paid visit to me, had been, of course, as predicted.

And that's the story of that.

Two years later...

Constiglione got in a fight in a bar in Manchester. He had been beaten up sort of pretty bad. We had to take him to a medic, where he was laid up for a week and a half or a week or so.

Also, One of Lady Vi's male consorts had ditched her at a restaurant. She was slightly broken-hearted after that, but she always had the Trinity to comfort her.

I myself, made it out, fairly well, sort of fine. My new ultra ultra-superior supreme mansion broke down three times, and had been later hi-jacked by a government trafficking agency.

As for the lamp, we had just lost track of it, after a while. We put it aside, maybe to come back to it later.

b. January, 1616, or 1617.

10

THE 1620S

story about China, India

Section i.

So anyway, about this time we had reached the 1620s.

Business had done well.

And we continued to strive for excellence.

There was an article on China, and then another one, on tea leaves.

China had recently got into a stick, which is a story I shouldn't bring up here.
We had gained several valuable collector's items.

Also, Constiglione had recently been recruited by a triad.

That's a gang, right? said someone.

Not really. It's actually more of a community reach out program, Constiglione explained.

I talked with their dai lo, briefly, once or a few times. He, Tiger Vang, seemed a very sullen individual.

The Story of Qu Solo.

Many, many centuries ago in Old medieval China, there existed a famous barbarian warrior, named Qu Solo. Qu Solo was also a strong wizard and a battle mage. He lived to be over two hundred years old. He was very good at architecture.

He walked hard, like a well built champion. And he was known for moving higher elements, like large fire and water, with only his hands and his mind alone. And much heavier items of wood and incredible metal, he could move them heavily, as well, with his arms. He had the strength like a master.

One day, the town had been ravaged by a series of powerful wind surf. Qu, 'Chu', still managed to defend his city well.

And he was awarded with loads and loads of money, and also he gained the very good support of two good looking pretty princesses.

What happened to him after that? I asked Vang. I also happen to speak perfect Chinese, of course, as well.

Qu went on a quest to start his own construction company, was the answer.

Thank you, Vang, was my answer, to him.

And that was our very rich conversation.

On to, tea leaves.

Section ii.

Tea leaves, Hanna explained, had an integral part of well used crown circles.

I smiled, peaceably.
I had been meeting with Hanna, at her temple, every eight years or so, certain centuries.

Left alone, the Tea leaves, often collect and take shape of a whole.

The four (or six) main symbols included:
The snake.
The rabbit.
The fox.
The stone.

And also, these four others.
(5a) The goat.
And, (6a) the house.
(7a) The bull

And, (8a) The star of paradise.

(1) The snake represents elements, of piety, and majestic piety. Of course, the symbol itself directs to symbols (quite often liquid), of change and transformation. The most popular, being, the raven or water raven. The raven was considered the ultimate.

(2) The rabbit represents elements of softness. The good rabbits were, of course, well-meaning symbols of love. They represent greater calm, and quite often, light benevolence.

(3) The fox, represents money, craft, economy, and speed. Also, this symbol acts kindly, and with greater, greater elegance. Systemically, the fox also represents enhancement, and good enhancement gifts.

(4) The stone, represents weight, heft, and solid dimension.
Example: We drafted, a map. The stone weight, acts, as a serious axis of strength.

(5a) The goat. The goat represents strength and ferocity. Later, they found this symbol was connected to certain mountain mysticism, and their beliefs, and their traditions.

(6a) The house represents, also, love and care. Love and care. Often, represented by a circle, or a cube, which due to similarities, are often connected.

(7a) The bull is, in Norway, and parts of England, and several other areas, considered a sacred animal, to be treated well. Quite often ranked with powers and potency.

(8a, or 9a,) The final match. The star of paradise (silver, or pink). For a length, this signal is often considered priceless. An angel. It indicates, the sail of the grand high priestess, symbol (and, of course, meaning, the heart).

"What was my symbol?" I asked her.
It turned out to be the fox and the bull, she explained.

Section iii.

India. 1628.

For a while, we rode through India. I bought a horse. Vi had packed breadsticks for me.
I chomped on a bread piece.

In India, bread is often soft. Then drank some water. Some for my pack mount too.

Vi had decided to stay in Delhi, for the trip. I was thankful that she even came along.

I surveyed the side area to the side of the road. I checked the map again.

Then, I checked with our guide, Hector.
It was still a very long way to the top.

After all that, I guess I appear very grateful, as well.

Section iv. 1632. Back in France.

Don't ask me why. Please don't ask me why right now.

11

THE 1630S

meeting with Richelieu

1631.

I woke up one morning to an important notice.

Apparently, I was sought for meeting with a very important individual, looking, of course, to conduct a heavy briefing involving military purposes.

The countries had been engaged, for the past twenty-five or so years, in a very large battle war, named as the twenty years war, which would become the thirty years war, over a decade after. Originally, this war was the battle for Protestantism. Now, later, it had become the battle against Spain.

They say we go to war in our sixties, and also, in our twenties.

During those wartimes, and this particular wartime, we still had to earn a sum peace rating, so they devised that I would meet with major power pieces as a diplomatic officer, during times of generalized pressures. I had worked my way up to the position of count, or deft military officer, earlier that year, and also many, many years before. They had introduced me as a war corporal, who had owned a large shipping warehouse, and who made several charitable contributing works to various, including several missions.

As mentioned, due to my high citizen status, it would be customary for me to hold meetings with very highly important individuals.

Clearly, someone had booked the appointment for someone else, I later discovered.

One of them, with whom I was set to offer meeting, had contacted myself about a very major celebrity individual of very large renown:

The major celebrity individual had, as I found out later, been a very highly well deemed cardinal (The new archbishop had been officiated at some point in this century.). To several great marks, he had unified a country.

His name was Richelieu. Patron Saint Richelieu.

I was to wear my military rank in his presence.

"Okay, Richelieu," I said to him. "Here I am, representing the second, or third, or fifth estate, and all right of that," I said.

"Yes, indeed," he answered. "Yes, indeed, as well. Quite honorable it is, and quite inevitably noble, to see from a very, very higher viewpoint, and from a more level plane as well."

"Good thing we booked some high quality survivors," someone in the background had added.

This seemed interesting to me. I had, recently been forced to sell, a good deal of good property, in order to deal with, and pay to, certain acclimating tax rates, in my country (of common stay) that year, of England and part of Germany. I did not mention this to him of course. They had been raising money for a great military, that year and twenty years before.

We sat on the promenade, well thought out. I took a large cracker piece, and bit into it.

"How is the good acknowledgement there?" he inquired.

"It's no big deal, of course," I said. "I am, of course totally grateful. It is truly an honor, great colonel Richelieu. I find your ops, and your taxation ops semi-brilliant, if you ask me. Not that I always don't always know, myself, of course, right? "

"Of course...," he said. "Taxation issues, and discussion are often quite seeming essential. However, quite important it is to acknowledge, and quite important it is to acquire a more moral clergy."

"More water for citizens, eh?" I said.

"Most certainly," he concurred. "More water for citizens, of course. And more for them, as well. Citizens, of course, need cx tra additional good corrections, and some very good diet, and some very good life aid, from time to time," he added.

"Darn straight. We have to maintain the good and direct course. No way should we have to pay them more than extra, to pay for more than extra, to pay for their local funnel pit. They get more than enough of that dough, and way, way more. I'm telling you, that money is, and should be, as good as ours. I give my approval. I give way total approval." I added quickly, which I included, for business of state purchasing.

"Now, of course, now, of course. Of course. Obviously, Military, and military ownership is important, as you made. Also, as mentioned, we must of course, express obedience for military and state matters," he continued.

I rooted him on, for this, in fact:

"And military dealership, I might add. That's right: If you owe the state money, you pay them, you effin' pay them. You effin pay them, right now, man."

He seemed very contemplative for a moment. "Yes," he said.

Here we were, not at war at some points, Richelieu. As it seemed. And we agreed. I totally agreed. I was quite surprised, and impressed.

"I totally agree," I said again. "I gen. try to take care of it myself, in fact, in that, too."

"You do not seem that bad to me," he admitted.

"Good advice," I said.

"We represent the Immortal, in fact, sometimes, I think," he added.

"That we do," I said.

He nodded. "Yes," he said again.

"These are, by the way, some really great bread snacks," I mentioned.

"Thank you," he added, and that had, of course been our meeting.

Afterwards, someone spoke to me in private later, and I accepted some quick licensing i.d. with them.

And thanks.

I stayed in Bordeaux for over a year and a half after that.

12

THE 1650S

lightermann attends new world conference

1650.

There was an article about the new world state conference. We sent lightermann to attend that year, to act as a representative, probably because I really didn't want to go myself, and I didn't want to get us shut out in the future on this one. Lady Victorian had a fit when she heard I might not attend that year, and so it became a tour for all three of us, lightermann, and Lady I. and me, for that year, at that point.

For the past eighty years or so, there had been a slight ruckus over the issue of a very, very large scale land deposit, owned somewhere in the east, in theory. Later we found out this theory was sort of inaccurate. It all lay to the West of ours.

The New World State Conference was held in Berlin that year.

One of the first speakers took the front.

A man by the name of Oris Czhecklander.

Czhecklander had devised a quick shift mode list, of important dates and times. Currently the world was in need of highly specialized products. He announced.

Based on certain prior events, he had entailed certain other events could be predictable. With time, as an instrument, he included, and evaluated.

At rate of going, population speed might largely increase, at the moments we reach at 1712. He pinpointed this number as an important date, in which he figured the world may reach a certain plateau. He listed some other important dates.

1858.
1633.
1904.
1780.
1870.
1971.
2049.
2118.

Quite often he seemed a bit of a chronologist.

For the benefit of the world, he said, he included.
We all cheered.

And that was his presentation.

The second event speaker, happened to be a female speaker. Her name was Opal Tanenbach.

She demonstrated a remarkably good fashion sense, and an intelligent smart management skill presentation.

A very high quality round of applause, came after.

The third event speaker, was announced:
Vandergaard.

"That's you, Vandergaard," I said to lightermann.
Lightermann made his way up to the stage.

"Go, hon. Go collect your rewards," said Lady V.

"I want to give my presentation, good," said lightermann.

"First off, I would like to thank, audience for being here, at my great award show. I Turned out to be very pleased," he said.
A good-looking blonde woman smiled at him. She must've thought him, lightermann, to be very good-looking and cute as well.

"To orchestrate good agenda, I will actually give my presentation here. *Goood.*"
He took out a series of graphs and importance mappings.
"In this demo, I will actually show you two new important tables."

"The first table represents good drawn numbers, connected with..., 'pause' good theoretical incline. It demonstrates lift-up, versus spin. And light pressure. To do the world more dy-namic, we must initiate proper acreasement levels. And motion.." Acreasement? No matter. He was clearly trying to illustrate a correlative value, involving light effect, and speed physics?, maybe, probably, maybe.

"The second chart, represents cost ratio. Illustrated: The good world makes sense, will bring down costs, effective. Markets rise. For tomorrow. We saved. Proper. And good world issues. Isles speed up way. To make good way for good progress. As more devices are added, so adds rate of evolvement. Money marks sale. Thank you." This is somewhat more interesting to me, this chart. Lightermann has made this statement at least thirty times in the past ten years. He was trying to illustrate that, 'Good travel makes bread.' Or something similar.

"Finally, that's all." He said.
"Very good-looking, you guys," he complimented the audience.
"I am Vandergaard. Thank you," he said again, concluding his presentation.
The female speculators seemed in love with him. Clearly vandergaard (lightermann) would make the world money some day.

Very good. Lady Victorian clapped, and I applauded.
"Bravo," she said. Bra-vo.

The fourth and fifth presenter did an article on castle-grown hemp. Seemed interesting, I'd considered.
There were four or six other presentations, after that, for that

day. I took careful notes on all of them.

After that, we went out for some bratwurst, and stuffing at a local dine.

"So what did you think of the events?" I asked one of the attendees.

"Best one ever," he told me.

A few of his group seemed very satisfied.

Some extra notes.

Someone wrote in to me.

The letterer inquires:

Q: Was Vandergaard, or 'lightermann' ever a member of the Trinity?

A: Yes, in fact he was. He was considered the fifth member of the Trinity for a while. We renamed our group shortly after Hanna left our circle, which occurred: her departure from, around close to the late eighteenth century. I'll talk about this later in another chapter probably.

Q: What was the new name of your circle after that?

A: Actually, and obviously enough, we called ourselves Team Five. Pretty clever, right?

-Herkomar

Thank you for writing in.

My main man.

Also...

Re: Conversation, in earlier chapter:

By the way, I feel I should lightly apologize, to modern readers, for some of the reactionary elements, of the language used, in the chapters proceeding this one. I myself have been known for liberal cause, at a certain few points in my life. However, stricter mannered times, as are called, more often call for very heavy conservative and highly rational demeanors, of myself, from time to time. I still feel honestly about taxes. I am, of course, a conservative. Crucially the state supports its servants.

I honestly believe this.

13

THE 1670S

article involving muskets, age of piracy, visit to Spain, England

The earliest known handgun had been developed sometime in the year 1496. It was manufactured, as they say, close to Italy. A few records go earlier.

To mention:

Flash powder had, of course been, a German re-invention, invented by a Grey Friar, around 1313.

The instructions were made very simple. Add a dash of sulfur, and some charcoal; mix with concentrated alcohol, then dry; and, to a pile and a pile of saltpeter; or, for non-display: add, to a pile and a pile of smooth potassium carbonate, which I found, later, in the latter half of the very next century, worked better, faster, and louder. Supply well, with some additional cotton or wood cellulose; handle within reason; and enjoy the results. After that, a spark will do. Boom, goes a grenade, they say.

There holds records that pre-date and post-date this discovery, around the 1200s, by the Chinese, and the late 1600s, when, mixed with metal shrapnel, the combined mixture of concentrated flash powder could be used, reportedly for purposes of serious warfare.

Important, and somewhat obvious, note: The actual birth of the Renaissance, or 'the Rebirth', coincides with this period, as I suspect most already knew.

And there we were in 1671, holding muskets and hand cannons.

I loaded the bullet.
I took aim. And the round went off.

It smacked, very light, against the rockstone,

"They're building better arms these days," I mentioned.
Constiglione said nothing.
"Do you think it might be time for us to settle in a new area?"
"I'll probably stay behind," he reasoned.
He drank from a cask of punch.
"Maybe," I said. Someone has to keep tabs on our property, I figured. Constiglione always stayed clean.

"Still, it's a whole block of land, all to ourselves."
"And the situation with the *indios*?" he asked.
"They sound fairly innocuous, if you ask me." I answered.

I had heard a report on the issue, involving enslaved Native Americans.

"You should really consult Hanna. On that issue, if you decide."

"Of course. She should maybe know about that too."

"Who would you be taking with you, by the way?"

"No one. I thought I'd go myself." Maybe. More recently, I'd preferred being alone.

"Yes, I thought you'd say that," he responded.

Pause.

"Well, good luck," he said.

"Thanks. We'll see how it goes."

"Why don't you take vandergaard?" asked Constiglione.

"What? What?"

"To the new country, I mean," he said.

I thought about this for a bit.

"Maybe. Maybe."

Change subjects.

"So, anyway..."

"So how's your wife, Constiglione?" I asked him.

"She's not my wife," he answered. Recently one of Constiglione's new models had managed to seduce him.

"Penelope?"

"Yes, she's such a doll though," he said.

"I can imagine."

"Like Ellaina." He said.

"Cor," I said. This meant 'of course'.

Politely.

"How is Hanna, by the way?" he asked me.

"What?"

"Hanna. How is she?"

"She's fine," I guess.

I hadn't seen Hanna in a while though.

It was getting to be about time I booked another appointment, with her.

Change subjects again.

"And the picnic festival that you attended?" I asked.

"Last month?"

"Yeah."

"It wasn't bad," He said.

"Did you join them?"

"Not really The picnic seemed moderately enjoyable."

"Is that right?" I had attended a month earlier.

"That's right. Sort of." He paused.

"They picked another set of keys for you, I heard."

"Yes. Yeah'," he said, he meant. He handed over a spare.

Thanks. I lit a helpful cigarette.

We tested the pistols, once more.

I took the set of weapon, when I went.
Solid was the hand cannon. And I felt slightly more involved.

They say, Here marked our futures.

Later...

Also, an additional section: The Age of Piracy.

Sometime around this period, the 1680s, we were dealing with a major resource surplus. This section may not be included in certain history time books. However, I myself was there, and I do remember this happening around this time.

There was a slight and sudden increase, in product and a very sudden increase in intelligence, and product intelligence.
During one of the Earlier Ages of High Travel, apparently what entered the markets, was a high range of improved gift and spice products. Sellers stocked in boxed product. Spice products, once again, hit the roof, for the fourth century in a row. Together, they all seemed great.

Also, Included in the demo, was a quality density opium product, which was found readily available to be bought in extraordinary high qualities at the opium store. Smoked properly, the item was referred to as madak. I myself refer to this item as 'malak', with an

L', which was mixed with tobacco, brought over from the States, and been sold in Jamestown, later called the americas. The price of products, and malak, went up as well. Instead of buying less, of course we still bought more. Wealthy individuals, of course, knew true value. Market value had skyrocketed.

Lightermann's prophecy had actually turned out to be correct.

After a while, my self, as described, I had become quite more and more enthrallingly addicted (to products), and feeling more and more incredibly intelligent afterwards. Intellect skyrocketed, as well. There was, of course, magic, in consumption of products and materials.

Even I myself had entered the market on this one, even at a certain point, and made a small mint fortune off the dealing. Consumers wanted more. And I wanted more. F--k the Age of Piracy, we thought. We'll just buy more and more consumer products. Which I stocked, compulsively. And that was the result.

Our consumptions had well affected all other markets, it seemed. The economy ascended. All good, and all goods, seemed to increase, particularly, the products that we loved: Opium.

Lady Vi had used opium products, excessively, and even way more so than myself or any of us. For, she had been convinced that the product enhanced the incredible arts of the Immortal.

On my visits to her, I would often carry some opium, as a gift.

Sometimes I carried opium or madak, or 'malak', wherever I went.

For mine and hers.
And for Greater.

Generally, for a while, I would not go a day, or even a waking hour, without opium or some form of tobacco. It had proved a good luck charm. Women looked in my eyes, and found me imperturbably very attractive, they'd describe. And they had been fond of opium, too.

And always, it seemed to satisfy them.

Truly an age of greater security and heroism had prevailed.

Tobacco, from the Americans, as well, of course, had also truly, truly loved the Immortals. It's true, they would always always always be loved. And here, was our clear evidence. I could be away, for over ten years in another country, and precious malak would still be there, and still be there for me. The book that Hanna had given me, over a century ago, had been largely, a good guide on how to handle medicinal product. This book, had turned out to be correct, as well.

It helped me clear all my souls.

Good good good, soul.

After that...

1683. I met with Hanna, on the while. She had seemed very busy.

"Don't talk to me, right now, Herkomar," she said.

So I left.

1685. And then I fled to Spain.

What's there to do in Spain.

Not often. Spaniards are sometimes not really inclined to travel, in some areas. Quite often they visit England. And other parts of Main Europe. They had the past few decades exploring new world areas across the main ocean.

Besides from that, they don't generally go southern.

I spent three and a half years in Spain. Touring markets, and meeting with some of the more attractive, good-looking young blonde women, of Castillo.

I searched some of the articles of Spain in the meantime, as well.

Historians Greater Archive:

Many, many years ago....

I remember reading this report, way earlier. I kept the article on his findings. Included was a map to the Newer World.

Someone else had been following me, so I folded the papers, quickly, in my portfolio keeper, for good luck, I guess.

Apparently another one of theirs had already made a long journey across. His name had been Coronado. This had been the earliest I'd heard of him, however. I had read about this in one of their reading finds, which I discovered in the archives section in someone's private library, held in upper Madrid. Over ten decades previous, 16th Century legend, Spanish hero Coronado, on the search for mystic realm, had led certain expeditions covering cross country, in the newly discovered continent. He seemed partially a genius, in fact.

Of course, I used more opium products while I was there.

And also, I conducted further research on literature.

17th Century Greater Archive:

Someone had written an important book, back when, entitled: Destined for Theopolis, published in 1664. Partially non-fiction, the book delved on matters of future high relevance, including transformation of future wind shape and theory. Also, the book went on to discuss option parameters of time travel. Time travel, was speculated, to hold at least six or more individuals. Set forth, the extra additional theory that possible item variables in the past or future could not be changed or altered due to concretized spec. Otherwise, the time transport itself, would not know where to receive.

The book did not last long on the market, and eventually vanished entirely from the market, half a century after my reading, I later discovered.

To discuss for later, maybe.

Then a tour of England.

I had met with Lady V. numerous times that afternoon. Her bright talk was of peace treaties and good order maintenance for her rightful province. Dazzled, I thought of her. She left me with a pleasant long hug.

To strengthen our relationship, she figured.

And also....

And by the time that we had approached, 1688, we had reached the next chapter, of Herkomar's book.

14

THE LATE 1680S

colonialism, currency, they settle on america

Spain and Portugal had been annexing territories all over the new world, it seemed. Apparently, also worth mentioning, a Dutch company, had also recently made a non-suspended purchase of land (New Amsterdam), as well.

The land had seemed inexpensive. Several of us were eager to get in on the new territory gains.

It was important, I realized, that I had to make some early claims on the new continent.

For who did you represent?, a woman asked me later.
What?, was my response.
For which country was to support you on this venture?, she asked again.
I was to support myself, I explained to her. I always totally support myself, on basically every item I conduct.

Herkomar, is Herkomar's own master !!. Got it?
Then I gave her a hug. She was cute and very pretty and blonde.

I prepared lightly. We had to prepare some good ships for our voyage across the main ocean.

Packed, were a pile of spice goods, I'd take with me, a wide range of preserved steak meats, and a range of fourteen important books, that I had purchased at auction.

Q: How important was the invention of paper?
A: It turned out to be very important.

There was a discussion over currency. Recently, with the advent of paper currency, influence and power became easily producible, by print.

After a while, cash money became more and more than common. With this development, all worthy countries would soon become richer, and the good and worthy citizens of each country would all be placed two notches or several notches higher, or far, far higher and greater than that, even.

There were, of course no major issues with that.
And No worries about the inflation rate, of course. No one needed to. They'd just reset the level. And we'd all prosper again.
We had paper money to be taken care of.

For a while, It seemed as if the world would be owned by the printer press (and by those little slips of paper.).

German accountants would simply walk around town buying up whole entire shops and properties. Everything after that, seemed government-owned. Restaurants were government-owned. Women were government-owned. Even the inn and the salon were government-owned.

This, of course, had all been good news for me. The solidification of the country was highly important. The birth of modern nationalism had come in at around 1408, but this much more recent development was very important, for me, as well.

Like I said, The new currencies soared, and we all prospered, and felt protected. I checked with one of my sources, and after that, I knew we had it made.

Constiglione would, of course, benefit the most. He had managed to make some very good and brilliant transactions. And Vi and me, we would take a huge score from this, as well. I had to sell a property or two, but I knew a few individuals who'd have the papers to cover it.

Also, I had another tremendous hoard, which I always knew would be kept safe. In situations, I could always run back to my older precinct, to dig up a huge wealth or two, or ten. I had more than enough. I had more than enough to cover us all for the next two hundred decades, if need be.

What we had, in the cash, we were all looking to spend, high notes, and accumulate.

The banknotes, we set aside, and would always be worth value.

And, By 1692, we had made it on board to America.

Now,
Regarding America:

There was a friend of ours, we knew, who handled a large print-ing press, and had worked out of the Americas, as a printer of short novelties.

He, for the most part, was based closer to the North, and at a good plane.

Description of our journey across the main ocean:

In 1689. I brought, with me, several thousand good papers. To them, it might've made acceptable currency, I'd figured. I'd con-sulted a decent transactioneer. Also, I brought several items made of gold, which I stowed secured safely.

At that point, the plan had been, at that point, to settle in Quebec.

The ship we were booked on, was named Fast Jack's. It took us most of the way, and across the ocean too.

We had sailed in groups of three. Alongside, and in front, held, two other ships: The good ship Miller's, and also, The Orlleana.

The food had been very acceptable. I had booked first class sailing, of course. I however did not have much of an appetite for food or drink. For a while, it seemed a miracle that we even survived such a long and trying voyage across the North Atlantic.

Slightly I had been one to be affected by the rocking movement of the waters, which were very rough.

The waters and the winds had been like no others I'd experienced.

Thankfully, when we got off. We landed very close to Nova Scotia ('New Scotland'), or Acadia.

One of Lady Victorian's female friends had booked passage along with us. Some nights she kept with our group. Plus, there were two others, plus a female friend of my own. Also we did wind up taking Lightermann, along with.

By the time we landed in the new country, we were greatly comforted and relieved.

Q: Did you get superstitious?

A: About arrival? Not a bit. Not lately, anyway. I don't believe in superstition, sort of, or, sort of, not that much. Lady V. was a firm believer in luck value.

However, I must state, as a scientist, for any act of faith or magic, quite often there operates a magic science and a science value or magic value or ultra magic value or principle, that explains properly.

Magic often occurs based on reason, I later found that out.

In group with me, as mentioned, two of Constiglione's new models, the female friend of Vi's, named Teresa, and lightermann, and a female friend of mine called Sable, as well, as it turned out. We had all survived. The rest stayed behind. It would be me and lightermann, and three of four of our very good-looking female model friends, in the new country for the next two decades or so, at least, I figured.

There were six of us total. Among us, there were four females.

The new country, we knew, would take good care of us too.

Probably, I'd still miss Hanna. At some point, I suspected we might send for her later, if she ever changed her mind.

15

THE1690S

argument over printing press,
introduction of spade

Another advantage of the printing press, were newspapers. Originally founded in Mainz, for an early publication of the Gutenberg Bible. Decades following that, a series of gazettes had been published. Even the new world utilized this technology, we found, which, on arrival.

Through that, information could be preserved, and available to distribute in mass.

Interesting note: We handled the receipt of technology very well. These devices had benefited us goodly.

Early newspapers were printed on rough sheets of paper. News paper, we called it. And sold for basically a dollar equivalent, back when.

I searched on page one.
There was an interesting article on:
The Chaerokoi nation.
Apparently, they had listed several quotes.

"I never thought I had it in me."
-quote from, Lady Damascus, of Massachusetts

And also, an article on:
The Wallpost taxation issue, up five percent.

"Clearly, we're dealing with a land of free'd government...at this point."
-says William Winton (29), of Vermont

I considered the issue. The point had been made.

On 1694. We had been traveling a lot, and along the road to Hartford. We took a break in New Astrid for a while.

The air in America had been crisp and fresh, particularly in Astrid. We stayed at an inn.
Lightermann went through some of his pack items, on the upper floor.

Shayla and I ate at the local pub. A lot of the diet was appropriately, water, food and bread.

Section ii:

Inside the American pub:

The man, the new American, wore a long coat and a fine leather hat. He looked vaguely Dutch, with perhaps some very light French ancestry, as well. He also seemed maybe in his mid-30s, but I had barely noticed. Life had been decent to him, it seemed. He had a casual masculine friendly demeanor, and he beamed of a very high, very rugged intelligence.

Carrying a small bound text book with him, he introduced himself as Spade.

"The name is Spade," he said to me. He took off his hat. "You're one of the newers? Did I get that right?"

I handled him oblique and coldly. He had seemed a bit arrogant, to me. I had been reading a newspaper.

"Yeah. 'pause' Yes," I said. What's it, to you, I wanted to say to him.

Spade: "The townsfolk wanted me to introduce myself, to you is all."

"Uh huh," I said.

"The town, I should inform or I should say, is districted into three or five main areas," he said. "I myself work in the Fairmont district of King's. I happen to be a journalist and a writer."

I didn't ask to hear any of this.

"And the item of that?" I said.

"It means we're better," he said. "Fairmont is sort of our main company, or conglomerate."

"Why, a conglomerate?" asked Shayla.

"A collection," he answered. "Dunno," he said. "You two look very interesting though."

I said nothing.

"That's great," he said. "So, what are you two doves doing out here? You should be out. At the dancers place. Am I correct?"

I still said nothing.

"Okay, that's fine. That's fine. Look, if you don't want to talk, then we don't have to talk." He said. "I was sincerely trying to be polite. It was important that I log in a meeting with the two new-comers. You both seem very pleasant, in fact. So now we've all met, and that is all."

He finished off a large bread roll, with some salmon. And before leaving:

"It was nice to hold a meeting, you all," he said to me and Shayla. He dropped a text card, on our table, and two thirty five pence coins. "Have a very pleasant stay in America, the new country land and the new countryside," he added. And he paid his bill. Also, he paid for ours. At the tavern, and then he left. Adios.

We spent two days there, Shayla and I, and the rest of our crew. And then we were on our way to Hartford, via carriage.

And I had forgotten about my meeting with Spade. Modern Adventurer.

Around 1696-1699.

We bought some additional property by the ocean.

PART III

Modern Period
(late Colonial)

Modern Period (late Colonial)
1700s (the first decade)- article on hemp, their stay in america
1720s-Lightermann goes to college, Catherine the Great I
Late 1730s-meetup with Grey Fox, article on spade
1770s-older mage female (Hanna) takes exit
1790s-I Victorian builds an evening club

16

THE 1700S (THE FIRST DECADE)

article on hemp, their stay in america,

We stayed in Hartford for a while, close to Virginia.

Food, in general, we had eaten from cornfed livestock. Settlers had invited horses and rabbits to the new colonies, and also, several highly domesticated, wild, and domesticated livestock animals.

Even steak, was, for a while, found, and available, for certain buyers.

We purchased rich in American product. One of the spectacularities we had discovered had, in fact, been cannabis. Cannabis, and hemp, were widely used by ours in the state.

The cannabis plant proved fast-growing and strong enough, to support our entire household, the six of us, for over a month and over a year. Then we'd bought some more.

Cannabis, we had found to keep us warm, as well. When cooked, cannabis, saved decades of life.

I myself had invested heavily, in something I'd believed in, which could keep us level, and save the world for us, basically twenty-four-seven.

Some nights, we cooked it slow.

"So what's to happen afterwards," asked Teresa.
"I suppose we settle new areas," I said. "This land is very prosperous."
"Is it all good from here?"
"I suppose." Was my answer.
"Don't worry, I'll take care of all of us."
"Sometimes you know more about women, Herkomar."
"Sometimes. Sometimes, I care deeply."
Together, we smoked more cannabis.

The story of Teresa, at age fourteen.

When Teresa was fourteen, she started humming in her head.
Her friend, Ray, who was also, fourteen, began singing along with her.

"Why are you singing?" she asked, slightly embarrassed.

"I wasn't singing," said Ray.

"*You* were," he said, and continued.

When Teresa was eighteen, she won an award.

The Jay Roth Mastersons Award, given for excellence in artist skills. She had worked hard as an artist for at least two and a half years.

She took the podium.

"I would, most certainly, like to thank all of you." She paused a bit. She held the big metal sculpt, somewhat proudly.

She wanted to smile but couldn't.

"And I love you all," she said.

I sat back in my chair, and contemplated.

What if there were snow? What if there were sleet?

Would it be too much?

Would we have enough to make it through the winter?

I filled out a piece of paper, and placed another order for some more cannabis.

Cannabis was labeled a greater enhancement substance, and truly it enlivened our senses. Together, We'd pipe through a bowl of it, in less than an hour and a half. And grow stronger as a result. Our senses were well honed. Our metabolisms were at speed bolt level, after a while.

I had become a thunder god. Becky had become a valkyrie goddess.
She started to cry a bit.

It took some practice, but we quickly captured our levels.
We tried more, and more. And, For a while, it felt like we were floating.

Vandergaard, or 'Lightermann', he, had a not so great reaction to the root, but after two or three samplings, he had learned how to master the root plateau.

For most, he couldn't get enough of it.

For that, the cannabis root had been farmed from Jamestown, with the high quality Jamestown seal on the packets. Quality from a brand that we could trust.

I had managed to securely purchase twenty-two crates full, to last through the gorgeous winters in America.

How beautiful was this country, we thought. How beautiful was the snow, thought lightermann.

Cannabis, we still found to be more useful. It had doubled so many purposes, so many intentions, of life. The product seemed pertinent.

For the grand country.

The well-prized cannabis root,
Was...
as we were found.
Thanks.

Post: Quite often, they say that not much happens in the first twenty years. We did more and more cannabis, because of it.

1712. So there was our stay. In greater new America.

We settled in by the root, and I had purchased us a home.

The town seemed to play music quite often, and for the best.

The new country acknowledged greater rhymes.

We dwelled happily. Lovingly. Thrillingly.

Shayla, she said her name was. Her favorite color was indigo.

Everything was pleasant. For a good long, long while.

And with our great new purchases, which we had loved so dearly.

And we smoked more hemp. It had kept us all contained.

Thank you.
Quite deeply, we satisfied.

17

THE 1720S

lightermann goes to college, Catherine the Great I

I received a letter from Constiglione. Apparently he was dealing with a gold and diamond mining project centered around Dietrich, or Northern Praham., around 1723.

To Our Business,
I've been working on the project for close to two years now.
Evens seem to be operating fairly well.
Your female friend sends hugs and kisses, I'm sure.
I haven't spoke with her in two years.
They're closing down our business in two locations.
Your work is still needed, very optimally.
We have much to discuss, sometimes.
Someone is screaming over some field property right now.
Sorry,
(Jonah) Constiglione

Interesting, I thought.

I put the letter aside.

I sent a reply later.

And a thank you card.

We would, like to thank you.
Thank you.
Good working,
I guess,
I'm very sorry as well.
Very busy
Covering terrain.
Will make plans later,
To discuss.
-Herk.

And then we went back to work.

The women, we brought with us, aged gracefully, over the years.
It had been ten years later, and they all still seemed in their thirties,
and still beautiful.

Section i.

It came to a certain time that lightermann felt that he wanted
to go back to college. He felt there was quite more to life, for those
who went to college, more than a few times. This seemed feasible.
He looked around eighteen years of age at that point, and always

seemed around eighteen or twenty.

Q: Is that why you called him lightermann?

A: Yes, this is correct. We changed his name from vandergaard to lightermann, at around this point around the year 1726. Probably we initiated this change, because the new name, 'lightermann' sounded more collegiate.

When we had signed vandergaard, re-named 'lightermann', up for Yale College, constructed illustriously; we introduced him with the new name change. I introduced myself as his uncle. I myself looked around thirty-five, or thirty-six those years. I had wanted Teresa, to play the role of lightermann's mother, but, of course she had a fit about it, so I took Becky along with me instead, and had her play the role of my cousin.

Becky wore a cute colonial hat and outfit to the meeting.

For the record, this is how the session went.

"We were going through the slate," mentioned one of the board at Yale College.
"Is gud?" said lightermann.
A blonde woman nodded. She kept a good watch over.
There were at least two or three very good-looking femmes present, including Becky, of course. I, of course, introduced her as Becky.
"This seems all fine."

"How old is he?" someone asked.

"Nineteen," I answered. "And he's at a peak."

"Ja," said lightermann.

The blonde woman smiled. Lightermann had special influences and power over females, from time to time.

"Make a muscle for them, lightermann." I added.

Lightermann flexed. Lightermann, I was fairly certain, could bench-press maybe 12.98 times one hundred forty-eight pounds. Which, was merely decent. However, more importantly, lightermann was a very astoundingly good-looking guy, he was renowned for his good looks, which I knew would be more impressive to them anyway, and keep the women satisfied.

He looked very much like a modern day blonde surfer type.

"Did he test in?" asked an older gentleman, on the board.

"Of course," I said.

"Well, then that's what matters," he responded. "That's all I care about." "Tell your cousin, 'hello'," he added, solemnly.

"Then he's in?" I asked.

"Of course."

"Just, um...on your steps..."

"No problem," I said, and I dropped off a batch of check-notes.

The blonde woman seemed very intelligent. She winked at lightermann.

"He's cute," she said.

Lightermann smiled. He bit into a high-grain bar.

So after we had dropped off lightermann, we took the carriage ride back. It was mid-autumn. Becky held close to me.

Lightermann was to stay there for the next two years.

Section ii.

We visited him, lightermann, a few times after, while he was staying at the Yale House room.

"Okay, lightermann," I asked him. "What else did you learn?"

"Much," was his answer. He said, "Lightermann learned very much."

I had presented him with a larger-sized, late J.F. Fustbinder style, limited edition printing chapbook. A gift from a female friend of ours that year, the chapbook had been specially delivered, couriered over from the European market.

"Thank you," he accepted, somewhat non-receptively. He tossed it in his handbag, with subtle reluctance.

I checked over his roster. Some of the courses seemed fairly rough.

A series of textbooks were granted. He had brought a few of his own course books, which were listed on a bunch of tracts. After a while, I was impressed. Notably, he held a fair degree of knowledge about Christian right-hood, and several noble status high gradations.

"I have to study," he explained.

However. Fairly content, he seemed. Slightly more bookish, was his demeanor, in fact.

A woman gave him a kiss. He mentioned this to me later.

Well, fine, that sounds all right.

Section iii.

We played cards, to pass away the time.

I smoked another article of hemp. For a while, the world became quite gorgeous. Astonished, at our life value, we were.

Truly, there was bold uplifting, and we enjoyed every moment. For a while we missed lightermann.

Section iv.

So anyway, there was another article, I had to deal with, which is the article on Catherine the Great, which I include here.

Catherine the Great II, served as the beloved ruler of Russia, and empress, for over thirty years. She was born in 1729, and apparently, went on to join rulership title close to July 1762. She was, beloved, as mentioned, for several reasons. Catherine was known to treat well-class, very well, and freed them from various situation of forced servantry, compulsory, to the new state military. This I thought was fine, and acceptable. Also, She had proven an astoundingly prolific, high individual, of good worth, and beneficially, the writer of several literary works, and theatrical literary work, as well.

She, as a ruler, seemed very pleasant, and supported, basically, by all the citizens.

I did get a chance to speak with her in person, on one occasion when I happened to visit her area address.

This had been after a later visit to the Incorporated Union of Russian State Titles. She had been around fourteen, at the time, so I had to behave myself. I not totally sure as to why I tell this story in this particular chapter decade, however, I needed a convenient spot to drop these notes in, and this one seemed as good as any.

1742. Russia. Benson Wild State Party.

"You seem very quiet," she said. We stayed on the balcony.
"Yes. 'pause' Catherina, right?" I asked her.
"That's right. You were the guy who did the intro favor tour for that Scottish group handle," she mentioned. She seemed a very decent listener.
"Yes. Yes." I had wanted to change the subject. A pause. "Anyway, good luck with the country, hon. It all seems...very great." I said to her. I took a quick drink of cider.
"I thought that was very well honed," she commented.
I paused a moment. "I know. Yes. Yes, or somewhat," I agreed.
"What, did you find with the works?" she asked me.
"Nuh. What I found with the works, is effective management, and effective management and keys."
"Uh huh." She said.

"All you really need to do is, is hand out lots of good surplus wares, to wealthy esteemed individuals. Look out for those in the higher end. And champion for those in the higher end, sometimes. You still get it, right? Two, keep everyone sort of satisfied. Also, tell them, or...you can remind them, that the country statehood still loves them. They all still love them. I myself don't handle with those particular signatories any more. But that's what I remember."

She nodded, slightly, and then smiled. I blew a light party favor.

"Anyway...," I said. "So you'll do well, hon. And good luck with the writing. It's sure to impress."

"Thank you." She said, very politely.

And then we went to entertain the different separate parties, or crowds.

And that was it.

additional section., extra additional

1761.

And:
There were also some investigations in Lower America.

There were several large tracts of land, which we later purchased, from (and using) our own American scouts.

The fields turned out, quite plentiful, was the report. Cola had been a very good discovery.

More than five decades later. And in Later Colombia, and also Venezuela.

And, always we wanted more.

End of chapter.

18

THE LATE 1730S

meetup with Grey Fox, article on spade

1738. America.

I was called to business, and some point, in July; there had been a situation, close to modern day Alabama. A change-ling had been found, I'd been informed.

"Is that right?"

"Yes," said Holland, one of the messengers, from town. He passed me the notice.

I had an assorted reputation as an informed scientist, on the subject of human transformatives and also repair.

For the past four years, we'd been buying southward.

I told them, I'd take a look.

Grey Fox, just from looking at him, was the type of guy that Lady Vi., would've liked a lot. He seemed over eight hundred pounds of pure solid muscle which doubled to over 1600 pounds of pure solid muscle, when in wolf form. Also, he was very handsome, as well. His skin clearly glistened, when in human form.

A very good-looking female doctor specialist, Miss Pelov, looked him over, and examined his body. She had been completely enamored. Pelov also reasoned him to be of supreme condition good health. For a very long while, she seemed very highly, highly particularly impressed by his incredibly, incredibly gigantically muscular physique.

Maybe. I thought to myself.
I contemplated taking him back to Europe, with me, as maybe a present, for Lady Victorian, maybe.

I spoke with him in private, later. Again, for the most part, we discussed greater world health and technology issues regarding commoners strife and better newer civil formula enhancement.

Also, included:

Vaguely, he, Grey Fox acted polite.

For a bit, I told him the story of lightermann; and furthermore, I recounted briefly the story of LeVay, to which, I mentioned to Grey Fox, as well.
He, for a moment, seemed mildly uninterested, regarding both of those.

Anyway....

Grey Fox's own story, which he recounted to me, turned out to be one of astoundment.

Eighteen years prior, apparently, he and his brother, Cubby, had been out on a raid for drink and food, of a practiced Spanish-level settlement camp, back west. He had been only fourteen at the time. His brother had been eight years old. Noting their apparent youth, the Spanish settlers merely fired a few rounds in the air, as a warning only; and Grey Fox and his brother ran off. They had managed to escape, with two bottles of drink, and a tray of biscuits, which they shared.

Later, that night, they were attacked by wolves. Cubby had been almost killed, and very close to incapacitated. Grey Fox had escaped with a few minor bruises, and a large bite across his neck where one of the master wolves had bit him. He, Grey Fox, cried for four days over the loss of his younger brother. He abandoned Cubby, still breathing, by a wealthy white Spanish settlement camp, in hopes that they would treat Cubby's wounds, and raise him to live well, as Grey Fox had always hoped to live.

"Did you ever find out what happened to Cubby?" I asked him.

"Yeah, he eventually married to some Spanish girl, at the age of fifteen. I visited him a few times, after that. He doesn't have wolf powers, like me though. I'm sort of wanted by the law out there, so, actually, I don't visit him that much."

"Did you get married yourself?" I asked him.

"Nay, I found I really didn't have the time. But there were numerous very good-looking women. As usual."

Grey Fox then checked the time of moon.

He continued his story.

After the incident with the wolves, another interesting aftereffect happened about two and a half weeks after. Grey Fox had gained the ability to transform, into a wolf-like god-like man, at night when the moon came out. He'd grow to be at least three or four feet, or six or eight feet taller during transformation.
His body grew stronger every day.

Also, early on, after the initial wild wolf attack, he had found that he was possessed by a wild wolf god spirit.

Did you attack anyone? I asked.
Not really, he said.

Although later, at some point after 1730, he confessed to me that he actually did. On a rampage in his early days as a changeling werewolf, under very recent possession by the changeling wolf spirit, he had once battled an entire party of eight, of his own kind, in his self-defense, including two puritans, an American Indian field marshal, who had shot Grey Fox twice in the chest, with a hand cannon, and a Spanish-level deputy who came from around close to New Louisiana. It sort of didn't matter, at that point, seeing how I had confessed, to him, of my own light involvement in the Hundred Years' War, and also, in the later Crusades, in which I had won more than share of at least four of T****** descent, and at least two others before patching that issue up. We both had our sorrows, I suppose.

"Which Crusades did you fight in?" someone asked.

The Seventh and the Eighth, I answered.

"You were alive back then?" Grey Fox asked me.

Man, 'pause'. I am an Immortal. Some of us live longer, I explained to him.

Later, after two months of involvement with the wolf spirit, Grey Fox explained, that he had learned to talk with The Wolf Beast, as he called the Spirit that kept him under possession.

"How'd you do?"

"I simply offered him reason," said Grey Fox. "I'd explain to him why, certain options and certain reasons were better, and, he, The Great Wolf Beast Spirit, was always impressed. It didn't matter how insipid or weak my explanations were. The Wolf Beast was always impressed by reason, any reasoning, basically no matter what. After a week and a half of talking to the Spirit, he was so impressed by me, that he allowed me to re-take control over my own body, plus, given with all his additional power, and he left me with that, to my own accord," explained Grey Fox.

"After that," he said. "I was able to hold large transformations on my own business. Whenever I wanted. Whatever I wanted. Full moon, or none."

"Do you still communicate to the Spirit Gh*st?" I asked him.

"No. My body, is still all mine, for good nowadays," he said. "It seems," he added.

We had lunch for a while.

"How would you like to come with me to Europe?" I asked him.

Grey Fox seemed reasonably interested, but not incredibly interested.

"Maybe some other year then?" I suggested.

"Maybe. Maybe, that sounds good. Some days I'm more independent."

"We'll keep in contact then," I said.

"Thanks," he said. We'll keep in contact.

Section ii.

On my way out:

I left a five hundred slate, on the desk for him, to which he acknowledged.

Section iii.

After that, as mentioned, the plan was to go back to Europe, for more work. One of the old cadre, had sent us a notice, of a prepared annual meeting.

We were, of course, required to attend.

I was born ready to rock.

Section iv.

August 1739. On the Road to Rock Springs, Hampshire.

Also:

On my way, by wagon, back north. We still had to pick up light-ermann, and the girls.

I stumbled upon a good article of interest. This is actually a very, very good mention.

Written, in a very early early edition of the Philly Inquirer, was a notice on a former (quick met) acquaintance of mine.

Apparently, there had been an accident fire, in a district building lot, in upper Philly.

The fire was suspected to have been caused by a broken grease lantern. Blazed, the flames had melted at least three or four buildings.

Volunteers worked to aid the survivors.

During fire, one, a particularly brash young-looking hero, had braved in, and pulled out an additional three, plus a waitress and a bartender, from one of the burning buildings, which was used as a full service tavern hole, where the upstairs flooring had collapsed. He had also saved the lives of an additional family of four, from a conjoining building that was totally ablaze. There that man had proven himself a hero.

The character, of the article, had turned out to be a fellow roving reporter-journalist, a nice pleasant-looking man, it said: he, the hero, went by the name of Spade.

There, he had saved the lives of at least eight or nine individuals in one single night.

Appended was the note:

Spade has been identified as being over a hundred and twenty eight years old. Currently, he resides in New Jersey.

Most impressed, I was. It would always made me feel better. I had been once acquainted with the main hero of an incident.

I did not bother searching out Spade after that. I could've easily tracked him, but, However, I felt him entitled to his own well good life. What a hero, he turned out, man. Wow, again, I thought. Later, and some day he'd read fully this article. Maybe.

That being said, I'm glad the matter worked out for that. The world always needs good brighter champions.

There was a whole greater plane of adventure and stability ahead of us.

Thank you.
-Herkomar

19

THE 1770S-OLDER MAGE FEMALE (HANNA) TAKES EXIT

After another twenty-five years or so, when we all safely back in Venice. Vi, of course, looked great, as if in her pristine mid-late twenties. She held me tightly, which is more than I could say for the rest of the crew.

Constiglione had punched me lightly on my return, back home. He was still angry over some other situation, I suppose.

Still, there we were reunited, as the Trinity, with even lightermann, as a spare. Lightermann had gone to work on some of his own projects. He attempted to build a submersible, street auto mobile, of some sort, but he couldn't get it quite working. Water kept leaking in, he complained to me later.

No matter.
Again, we traveled the world. The four of us traveled the world.

Lady Vi.
Russia, 1746. Moscow.

By, The Palace of the Main. The Heightened Square had shifted slightly.

We stood outside, the larger palace. She wore her blue silk outfit that night.
I held her close, and comforted her.

"Vi..."
"Yes."
"Vi, You look so totally gorgeous, in this light."
"I know," she said.

All Through the Night.
We kissed like lovers.

Constiglione. Stockholm. Sweden. 1768.

"Constiglione,"
"Yeah?" he said. He looked dolefully away from me.

"I've been going through this book...." I said, I flipped through the pages easily.
"Right," he said.
"It seems there may be a cure for that underground administrative condition, you were talking about."

He threw an orange at me, full.
"You m*****f--ker," I said.

Lightermann. Still, he looks nineteen.

Canterbury. England. 1861.

"Lightermann," I said. "As I said, I still don't get how you expect this thing to work."
"Works submersibly." he said.
"Great."
"You pour the grain in," he tried to explain to me.
"Yeah," I said, yeah.
"Fire burns it."
"I gotcha…."
"This heats rotors." He said.
"Uh huh. Uh huh."
"And that, causes movement."

He loaded his contraption into the underwater tank.
The water kept pouring in.
"The water keeps pouring in," he asserted.
The water kept pouring in.

I have to put an inclusion in here. Lightermann is, like, our side-kick. Good-looking women think he's totally good-looking and cute and intelligent.

And more. In addition.

And also.

Hanna had booked a meeting with me later somewhere around the year 1777.

I hadn't seen her in years, before that. I visited her in Norway, where she stayed for a few, with her late temple life space.

She had been looking more around sixty on those days.

"Herk...Herk..." she said, softly.
"Hannah...?"
"Herk...Herk..." she said, softly.
"Hannah?"
"It's time for me to leave, Herk," she said.

She seemed absolutely serious.

"To where will you go?" I asked her.
"Elsewhere," she responded.

I dipped my head slightly, then looked over. I wanted to cry. She noticed, those tears.
"It's fine, hon, it's fine," she said.

"Will you be coming back?"
"I won't," she said, firmly, yet softly.

"You are, of course welcome to use my library." she included.

"Any book in the library. I'll be taking some with me, of course."
She added.

Yes,'m., yes, 'm, I said.

And that was the last we ever saw of Hanna.

Sometimes I remember them all. Hanna.

Constiglione.

Eleanor.

Alice. Shayla. Becky.
And Cooper.

Lately, I go through a few of these names, and my eyes get slightly wetter.
I close them, solemnly.
And then I take a moment to myself.

Sometimes. Sometimes.
Sometimes we grow older.

And some say that I look around (or close to) forty these days.

20

THE 1790S

I. Victorian builds a club

By the time we entered the last decade of the 1700s, Lady Victorian decided to do some of her additional enterprising. With her vast sources of wealth, she opened three or four new businesses, which of course were the salons, primarily operated in England, but in various other locales, as well.

Young good-looking men would enter to find a plethora of very good-looking highly young female models.

To this, they would engage in acts of poetry and good intelligent verbal exchange. The women had several levels of expertise.

I had visited these salons on multiple occasions. Myself, and lightermann received several numerous invitations to join the club.

Always, The place was totally packed with good looking individuals. We'd take breaks for good and very good-looking wait service.

The amount of influence I held, was likeable. More often, we'd feel very privileged.

These were, of course private salons, and studios, open to good-looking wealthy clients. Quite often, Vi entertained celebrities, at her clubs.

"This is sort of interesting, you did, Vi."
I commented this to her.
"Yes, yes...., the service truly brings in." she said.

"Where did you get the idea for this?"
She kept quiet for a moment, and then spoke.
"It's the type of thing that's been a long time coming," she said.

"How's Hanna?" she asked me.
I paused for a moment, and I didn't answer.
"She left," I said. "I'll miss her sometimes," I added.
"I guess," she said.

"The clubs will continue to earn more and more money."
"That's great," I said.
"That's great."

Victorian handed me three passes to her private elite club.
Very good, she informed me.

I spoke with Constiglione later, about the subject. He had also been recently been invited to a networking fundraiser.

"Why aren't you attending the network group?" I asked him.
"No mood today," he said.
"You can also at least attend Vi's service," I mentioned.
"I'm busy," he said.
"What," I asked "What the F' do you think you're busy with? You're not busy, man."
He paused. He had been working on rebuilding a bicycle, of some sort. He paused longer. "I just don't have time," He said to me, sullenly.
"Sorry," I said, I took a drink from an imported water bottle.

"You know, you're a really good guy sometimes," he said to me. He did not look me in the eye.

I smiled and took another swig of light water.

Venice. 1794.

Our winter book had come out which we distributed and sold.

The Validities of Minos, published in 1794, read the cover.

I had gone through chapter after chapter, to make sure the book was corrected.

Lately, the book had been about seasonal arrays, and of that sort. Control of esteem dealt primarily with economy, the book entailed. About which, climate and principles of area effect, was also highly important factor.

Most off, I found this information to be slightly admirable, and very truthful.

The book had been bound in fine imported italian leather.

I had stayed for three years, at the luxury palisade rooms.

I had purchased a good flat in England, and it kept me contented.

For a while I figured I'd work on some old goods of sort, long bows, which had been very carefully constructed.

The days at the office seemed somewhat bland, but I processed the shipments fairly well done.

section iii.

Technology stats went up greatly this decade. That's another notice.

Also, I succeeded in entertaining some very good-looking women, quite often and from time to time.

Dinner with Cheryl:

"So, as long as we have all that...," she said.
"As long as we have all that," I said.

I smirked, light.
I took a plate of beef, and we had a good supper.

Lunch with Diane:

"So what do you suppose will happen at the battery?" she asked.
The battery location, she had been referring to the dockyards.
"Don't worry about it," I said.
"What?" she said.
"It should all stabilize, I know," I explained to her.

How good those years were to me.
And honest.

We reached certain high peaks of financial enterprise, as a growth economy.

Dinner with Samantha.

"The gardens on the roof, they need to be slightly watered," she said.

"I'll take care of it later," I said to her.
Reassuring.

"How many does that mean to you, when you're at work?" she asked.
"You generally mean more to me quite often, and at work, I suppose," I suggested to her.

section v.

id. 1797.

So, I woke up the next morning, feeling slightly doused.
Someone had sent me a note-card tacked onto the door.

It read,
Just new in town.
Meet me up,
Important.
Signed,
An old friend.
Diesel.

Interesting, I thought.

Now I wondered who had sent this note. I have known of very few old friends named Diesel.

There was an address on the back, at the Ridgeland Hotel.
I attended, at that address. Out of my own interest, I guess.

"Really?"

I asked the women seated at the desk. She was a total smart
reception member, with dark red hair, and a total intelligent body.

She paused, and went through her notes.

"There's a good client of ours, available to meet with you," she
said.
"Guy or girl?" I asked.

"A girl, then," she said. "Go check her out if you want."

I walked up the steps, upwards. Towering.

There had been several flights. I had trudged my way upwards,
as mentioned.

And when I reached the floor, I steadied myself. I paused. And
then I pounded on the wood door, with the knocker. Slight pause.
No one answered. I pounded on the door harder.

"One moment," someone called from inside. The voice. I slightly recognized the voice.

And then she opened up. And it was, of course, as to who it was.

She opened the door.

And there standing, in front of me...,
was, a very pretty blonde, Alexia LeVay.

PART IV

After Enlightenment

1820s-Napoleanic Wars, I Victorian gets knighted

1830s-invasion of Algeria, Brussels

1840s-(publication of Leif Sterling), a friend of theirs (constiglione) perishes close to Alaska

1850s-story about Herkomar (he spends time with a female friend), third tour of france

1860s-(???)

1870s-their version of a Western, with Grey Fox; lightermann goes back to college

1880s-story about Pakistan; camera invention, Herkomar meets another woman, plus additional

Late 1880s-discovery of Eiko, he proposes theory of immortality

1890s-read the time machine, studies in time travel, with I Victorian

-220 B.C.-Victoria and Herkomar in Ancient Rome

-880 B.C.-Victoria and Herkomar in Ancient Mesopotamia

2114 A.D.-lightermann teleports to the future

21

THE 1820S

Napoleanic Wars, I Victorian gets knighted

The news came well, an elaborate celebratory event we held, in great incredibly great high status, for Lady Victorian was to be knighted.

For her proper service as a grand field operative, and captain, and warrior, during the Napoleonic Wars, that had occurred slightly less than a decade ago, she was, of course, to be honored.

She had apparently won, at least three of four battles, on the battlefield all by herself.

I had visited her, on one of these occasions, eagerly to check her female art warrior style. At the battle of Leipzig, and again, at the battle of la Rothier, under the name she used, "Lieutenant DuShaw", I also attended. To watch her, Lady Vi., in battle, was epically glorious. There, she'd stand nobly, endlessly, knocking down a series, with her long shimmering sword blade in hand, swinging,

swinging across, putting double and quadruple hard sword knock against her scattered opponents, who dared fight and bravely run against her. Several men fought. She cut into them quite well. In honesty, she mowed them down, tirelessly.

All with me in the foregrounds, cracking up.

Blood rained rich.

Later, she admitted to me that she longed for these men.

For her service, she was to be rewarded.

1822.

At the ceremony, they placed the jeweled staff to her head, and she was properly dubbed.

She: Our Great Master Swordswoman. Sir Lady I. Victorian. The 'I initial in her name, had incidentally, stood for 'Isabelle'.

How stunning, she looked, totally, our gorgeous, dark-haired Lady I. Victorian. A white diamond-ruby wrap adorned her chest.

And afterwards, she celebrated.

Q: Okay, Herkomar, I read somewhere that the Battle of Leipzig, and also the Battle of la Rothier, were actually fought by German forces? Is this correct?

A: Actually, yes. They were primarily German, at that battle. However, they were also Allied Forces, as well, which included Prussia and a few other nations. Lady Victorian enlisted herself. And so she fought that era.

And, so they did. Just as I say.

Q: Why was Lady V. interested in this at all?

A: She hoped to win. As I described, she sort of did, once again.
And there were a lot of other reasons, as well. I'll remind you, that these battles were battles for our prize grand country. I am, of course, partially, German, anyway. It was important that we protected and defended our land status, as figures of great royalty, which we had descended from. We were, of course.

If you must know, it was primarily an exercise in new technologies, including new ships and bayonets. And cash as well, and art and building. The Big Two included Food and Warmth. The Big Four included Knowledge and Technology.
This was a big issue, these battles.

They were arguing over the fate of the world.
So we stood our ground, importantly.

And more of that, and more too, as well.

Now, also, additionally, a male reader wants to know...

Q: Just what exactly is Lady Victorian's intelligence?

A: Lady Vi's IQ is approximated and tested to be at least 172 or 173. On a scale of one to ten, Lady Vi, ranks to be a 38.8. She is always stunningly magnificent.

Section iii. the Legend of Beo'Roth.

The Old English publication, of this, was finally transcribed again, around 1823.

It deals primarily with a trapped senator, of sort. He is, of course, embedded to his throne. His legend is divided into two and a half parts, in which he must confront, of course, with four, or greater, challenges.

First, there is the obstacle with the gate-keeper, to who he presents, very lightly, as a very eager sport warrior. This is to say, he presents himself well. When tested, and questioned, he makes the prompt, and wins the high range.

Second, he achieves a certain degree of super weapon super-technology. For which he is prized, and congratulated.
His rewards earned, total, and total better.

Thirdly, he must collect rewards, and distribute goods and entertainments. To win, of course, his protections, the hero, Beo'Roth, must take his high selections and guard carriers. He selects, and demonstrates, to his regulars, wisely. The tribe compose songs to him, later, and to his inspiring great majesty.

Finally, and fourthly, it amounts to his defending his country.

To which he takes his hinds, at for a run.

And the point: To stand defensively by your king, will eventually prove the great hero, as well.

And that was the article on Beo'Roth. And that, years go by.

I eventually loved this publication. A few of my friends thought it a piece of garbage. However, the legend remains a classic in my collection, treasured, and as always.

Section iv. article on Grey Fox.

Someone asked another question, as to exactly where Grey Fox was, during all this. We had him shipped in for a closer bit.

1828.

He had, of course, proven himself to be a great immortal, as well. At a certain point I wanted to make sure he was recognized to the new European countries, and the occasional visiting Royalty, which we were among.

We dined with him at the Central Hall of London. He ate his dinners in human form.

Grey Fox always had a strong appetite. That's one of the reasons, I was fond of him.

I had introduced him, in 1824, to Lady Vi., who adored him; and to, Constiglione, who had already, year prior, written, completed a three and a half year study on the changeling summarizations, and on the grand wolfen transformations.

However, still, we were all five of us together.

Someone suggested that we change the name of our cadre to Team Four. She may have just been joking though, I assume.

Lady Vi still protected Grey Fox, intelligently.

And more.

The Story of Alexia.

Alexia, of course, had returned, which I mentioned in an earlier chapter.

She had spent over the past forty years, in a hotel in Amsterdam, where she held numerous. For a while meaningfully content, she underwent several orders, by high class society clubs. To which she became more involved, they say.

After a while, she took up reading again. She took up several studies, with a collegiate society. Mostly, she hosted for them, and read, for she was a poetess. For a while, she played piano, softly, as a night act for a music lounge.

The story continued.
A minor crisis had occurred, when a female friend of hers had

been under investigation by a secret police force. Her female friend, had been held captive, for which she struggled for her friend's release.

There was minor success from that, and after a period of championing, the issue resolved to peaceful accords.

During the aftermath, Alexia regained.
She had purchased a large tract of land, close to the main city, where she stayed.

She dealt investments in paper currency.

Also: During the late 1760s and late 1780s, Alexia had made a very good deal of money, a sizeable fortune, in fact.

And she ran to her dear old friend Herkomar, who was always proud to have her visit. They hugged, and kissed, and once again, they engaged in discussion.

As for if there happened to be another privately known situation, previous, she did not answer, and I did not bother to ask.

Alexia and I held some very good embrace.

So what will we do tomorrow, she said.
Tomorrow, of course, we were to go for good grant meeting, and well (and wealth) livelihood.

"I love you too, Herkomar," she says, afterwards.

So then the evening ran.

I took a nap;

Then went for water.

Also, ii:

Constiglione was working as a partner, in an issue that involved The Miiannae Trading Corps Divisional. l. light Operants.: Krklnd., Dellware.

I spoke with him briefly on the subject. They were lightly switching operations.

"We're going to Alaska," he, Constiglione, said. He had been referring to an expedition troop. They were to start from the Eastern side.
Apparently they heard more rumors of land prospect, from somewhere.

"That sounds suitable, quite suitable," I answered. I had known about these areas, slightly. I had never traveled there myself, at that point, for the most part. I worried sometimes, for him.

I had wanted to talk more about the subject, but he was already out the door.

1989. Texas.

Also, an important note about this chapter, which I include, as well:

In February 1929, in Lahoya, South Ami., or, CA, after an allegation made by a visiting French emissary, La Carr, Lady Vi went on to purport later, that she had never actually killed anyone, even during those times of war, even when she fought, and she fought very giftedly and very valiantly. Also, she also does fully admit that she does vaguely remember being there very strongly knighted, which she does have the medals to prove, and mementos to remember. I know because she posed with them, all the time, for those modeling magazines, she was so proud of all those medals. Later, she smokes a joint.

I think this is an interesting note. This quick chapter previous was the way I remember it though. Lady Vi, why did you not tell the total total truth about this, like I did?? -Herk.

Lady Vi. remembers, quite well, and can show, all the time, st any time, she says.
I was very pretty, she says.

Another note: Constiglione was actually one of my favorite friends from back when. He always knew how to manage money.

Constiglione was, of course, our prince. And, we cherished him always.

22

THE 1830S

invasion of Algeria, Brussels

1832-1839. A few events, and articles, had happened this decade.

France invaded Algeria, and occupied under French rule.

The districted county of Belgium declared independence from the Netherlands.

King Ferdinand II had declared himself the King of Two Sicilies.

A series of riots broke out in Brussels. This was a pivotal time.

After a worthy level of industry had entered, to invigorate new product keys, presumably, they said, high demand occurred over their highest quality private product.

The Revolution in Belgium produced mixed results.

In truth, which had been revealed, there had been a riot over commercial market goods. The way it had occurred, they felt it established something.

Mostly, this had caused a moderately higher degree of public combativeness.

Very over-intense, some say, and ballsy critical, but however, highly dangerous.

These actions led to a chain of events. Upsetting, this was, for an important reason. 'A major f--k-off', had later been ascribed. And to those other predictions, had just begun.

There they all thought, we verged on the overly cerebral. (That had been their newer prime.) To be generally honest.

We all knew this back then.

Those policing constructs were set up to save lives.

Also: For the next ten years, Algeria was held and occupied under orders from France. They lightly conquered the North. Trade embargoes had been halted.

It had been set up to be the new colony, some had assumed.

Eagerly, they, the Algerians, waited for additional commands. They figured they deserved the acquisition. Later, in actuality, they seemed very eager to pledge fuller support. A contact mentioned.

We worried slightly, over this. This stage and era, we earlier figured, had already come to a final completion.

Had we guessed inaccurately?

Lightly concerned, we later realized, over this speculation, this strong habit, of revitalized warfare. Maybe, we guessed..

They had been likewise, in fact , more attentive to this channel. Carefully, there was a mixed deliberation.

And:

Spain and Sicily were both united under the rule of a Sicilian king. He had remarried over to Spain. Later, I remember, he published a secret diary edition containing articles relating to finance and reform. I recall this very vaguely. The reviews had been slightly less critical. Perhaps, we realized, he had also been appreciating the new ideal, once again, soon.

To that, there was an element of remodeling, to suit the needs of the newer consumer-based lines.

For a while, more travel had been initiated, due to those other later developments. What would be the new future? Of this, we wondered.

It all seemed worth the venture, some had afterwards speculated.

We were uncertain.

End of Chapter.

23

THE 1840S

(publication of Leif Sterling), a friend of theirs (constiglione) perishes close to Alaska

For some of us may not remember, the Epic of Leif Sterling (1848), was only published in 1830 or 1841. I knew of no records of the book before that. Truth be told, if the Epic of Sterling had been published before the 1830s, then surely it would've been lighter-mann's favorite book.

The book, summarized, tells the tale of ancient Sumerian warrior, the battle-hero, Leif Sterling, and his epic quest throughout to find, the attainable miracle, of immortality. He voyages with a friend of his. Parts of this book make me feel somewhat very sad sometimes. And we cry for the miracle, he writes.

I paid very, very good attention to books. It was worthy of many several good notecards, and more. To these several sections that I had read through, several other chapters, for a very light gift, for a good looking female acquaintance of mine; In addition, I, however, don't remember several of those moments of those being in there.

But they, those other sections, are still already there.

Open in Leif Sterling.

1838.

I had a good friend who didn't make it.

When word came to me, on a Saturday.
Delivered by a messenger.

Sorry.
C. didn't make it.
Left due to frozen gan.
Once again,
Sorry.

I looked at the piece of paper for a moment, and tried to make sense of it.
After realizing, I fell to my desk plate. I started to cry.

It had been a note regarding Constiglione.

According to the notes, He had apparently expired due to cold tracts. He was somewhere around present-day Siberia, so they say.

I consulted the text status manager or open field registrar's office, immediately. And I checked.

"How's my friend?" I asked him.
"Your friend?"
"Constiglione," I pointed out.
"Sorry," he said. "He is no longer here. He has perished due to cold.", they apologized....

There was a discernible light frown.

When I mentioned this to Lady Vi., she paused for a very long while.
A very long pause. Unsure.
Then she hugged me. Long and hard.

For a moment, I thought that Lady Victorian would start bawling, right there. We both had dinner together that night. Lightermann was away, navigating in Sweden at the time.

We barely spoke.
"So what are we going to do?" she asked me.
"I guess. I'm not sure. I guess we make plans."

We ate a white cream vanilla pie together, at the rest stop.

I also contacted Alexia about this. She was working in New Phoenix, at the time, as a female guide representative and messenger for a small group of very heavy land traffickers.

What happened, she asked.
"I lost a friend of mine," I said.
"I had nothing to do with it," she said.
"What?" I asked.
"You heard me," she said.
That I knew.

And then she sort of excused herself, for she had to go back to work.

On some days I find I remember more and more, exactly.

I spoke things over with a female friend of his. Her name was Alice, too. Her name was Alice Rutherford.

He, Constiglione, had owned and designed many paintings. One of which, was a painting of a long crystal white rose. I'm not certain why, but the picture still makes me feel very sad.

And there was the picture of the woman in the white blouse. She bit into an apple.

How we mourned. We mourned for weeks and days. They cried for him, every night, basically, it seemed.

And that, they knew, meant very much.

We took another longer pause.

Bonus Interlude: Additional story. Encounter with a bully.

This is another scene that I remember clearly.

1647. After visit from an early Prussian dignitary.

At one point, some other word had got around. There had been an encounter with a bully. Someone had conned young vandergaard, or 'lightermann' out of his monthly pocket fund. Count Lazerhawke, as he was referred, had tricked and mastered our younger companion at a rigged game of poeldart. Poeldart was a later homemade-invented parlor trick game, requiring a board, a tap, a deck of cards, and a pair of common youth-knives. When played over currency, the game was devised clearly for a victim's bilking.

Lightermann had been crying about it all week long.

"But when to get the money back...?" he asked. He sobbed slightly.

"Don't worry about it," I said to him. I had been focusing lightly out the window. A young dark-haired women, in a tight blue courtesan outfit, had been in view.

"Vandergaard?" I said to him.

"Yes...?" he said. He had slowly been mastering the language, well enough.

"I will retrieve your money for you." I said to him.

Vandergaard, or 'Lightermann' smiled. He seemed pleased enough with that answer.

Within a week, I invited myself over, to Count Lazerhawke's large master-estate. And over, regarding: The real actual birth name of the New Queen's Land District Area Count, we found out later, had been 'B. Operant' Duke Jozhef Bertauk Kruebenhopf. They had sent him over from Prussia over half a decade earlier.

I had confronted the Count, over the issue of lightermann's pocket allowance. My plan had been to turn the deck, if necessary.

Lazerhawke merely grinned. He said something, very sharp, to me.

Over the years, I had grown to hate the man.

Two and a half games of poeldart later, and the Count had still unfairly trickered me.

I quickly became aware of his sneaky treachery, and guile. To note, I had been once gulled, I realized. I would not allow it here, I thought. And then, however, soon after, to my surprise, Lazerhawke had conned me of my fine sports jacket, my men's carrier, pocket-noter, and much more, a large silk wad. Also, at least 45 British pounds, I had seemed to be missing later, I noticed, as I stumbled back on the road to inform vandergaard, at our central main HQ.

To them, I would explain. There must have been a further option.

To word: We would revisit once again.

I howled bloody vengeance, loudly, mightily.

Once, we had informed Constiglione. The operation was to be corrected.

"But how?" he asked.

"The man is clearly a snake," I replied bitterly. I had been referring to Lazerhawke.

"B'uh huh," murmured young lightermann. Tears streamed from his eyes. He had been crying early that morning.

"This will be no big deal," answered Constiglione. He went over to check his calendar chart.

He retrieved a wood box container, and also, his premium gold sword.

They said.

Two afternoons later. Constiglione returned from a visit to Lazerhawke, with the money (somewhere over eighty coin), and also, a very slight meager bonus.

Lightermann seemed overjoyed.

"And how did you retrieve the money?" I asked.

"I had answered his, Lazerhawke's, call. And once again, bested him cleverly," Constiglione explained.

"And how?" I asked. I had genuinely wanted to know.

"At a plain game of cards," he responded.

"A fair game...?" I asked.

"Of course," he said, abruptly, slightly offended.

"Honestly?" I asked him again.

He paused, slightly irritated, and smiled, somewhat broadly. He couldn't help it.

After a bit.

"Surely," he said.

And surely, he had still defeated Lazerhawke.

Yaay!!, exclaimed lightermann.

End of story.

Also:

Back to when we were younger, I remember, as well.

1486.

In Lady Vi's third brand new co-op. And, After a good discussion round too.

"So what did you make of the new trade on this one?" asked Lady Vi.

"I thought it was highly sophisticated, at bargain," said Herkomar. I was fairly certain of this.

"We could have asked them about the more involved dealing, what the tech stat was," she said.

"Maybe," he said. He thought to himself for a moment.

"I mean, it could've made a good better maneuver, for The Trinity, behalf and have, and all," she continued.

"I guess." I mean, I agree.

"Enough of that, we could've had two fortunes all together," was her additional comment.

"Yet we bought this one for a good deal, anyway."

A light pause. "I thought." She said.

"And here, here we all are." he said. And, he took a swig of red juice.

I thought. "And here, here we all are," I said.

"May, of course, we still survive again," said he, Constiglione.

We had purchased the deal for two eighty hundred. We already had a somewhat unlimited advance. We three knew an excellent buy deal when we came one across, on that. She said. It had been a major purchase.

And then,
And then, we punched forward again.

All our brighter fond memories together.
What very good, what friends, I guess.
I know.
I said, I know.

And then he was gone....

Constiglione had left.

And I had slightly forgotten more.

part ii.

1838.

Lady Vi. went out for a night.
I went out to get some air, I decided too.

Somewhere, in town, a little girl, Cassie, was sobbing. An older teenage girl was crying herself out.

1838. Later in October or November. At the funeral held. In Ge'nosha. Two towns away.

For Constiglione, former friend and good friend to women.

A larger service, they presented.

A woman, probably another artists model, with bold fire red hair and pure white skin, stood magnificently. She wore bright ruby red lip color, and a shroud of pure black cloth. Her cold eyes, were the color of pure blue cobalt.

She closed the casket. And that was all.

An older woman wept.
An actor friend of his milled in the background. He started kicking at the grass.

I frowned again. And I said my goodbye.

He had been our good associate.

And Later.

Of course, to mention this: Constiglione was truly an established genius master.

He was a very brilliant artist and a very highly highly brilliant engineer.

He was our good friend.

And, we will miss him, always, and remember him, very, very dearly.

We all loved him, as an associate.

Thank him.
And, Thank you.

-Herkomar

West Sussex Hotel. 1846.

24

THE 1850S

story about Herkomar (he spends time with a female acquaintance), (their) third tour of france

Around 1850, I decided to go on another tour.

Some days, I felt more for methods of visiting the various states.

1851.

They had re-invented the countries. Russia. Prussia. Germany. 1852-1853.

For a while, I was a roving immortal.

I traversed the streets.

A good looking dark-haired woman shared a garden with me.

This slightly comforted me, somewhat.

Lightermann was still away in London, those years.

I walked, and walked further.

Alexia had sent me a note that year. I guess she felt sorry for me too.
Probably, she remembered what it was like.

Maybe we'd attend a concert together, was the suggestion.

The years went by.
Tick tick tick.

Whatever had happened...?
Tick tick tick,

At times, it seemed as if I'd grown slightly more nonassertive, maybe.

Also, for some reason, I felt I should add a section on Mozart. The man saved at least two nations, is what I have to say about that. As referenced to, 1782

For a while, we both listened.

We attended a bar cafe in Holland. Alexia and I stayed there for a good eight hours or so.

Holding a large glass of cold cider. The best I could find.

And the world keeps moving,...

Tick tick tick.

Also, I spent more time with her later that decade. Our darling. I asked her again in 1855. She had wanted to go engaged, for a while. I told her, I'd think it over. Maybe later, I decided. Alexia. Sometimes I loved her.

In 1974: Years later, and we still didn't get married.

In 1856. Instead, we toured Paris together. She was partially German, like myself. I knew this already. Hanna, in the past, always referred to me as a Switzer. Together, Alexia and I, we toured the great museum hall The Louvre, in fact., classic. We had attended as private guests.

It wasn't exactly the same, but there was still some fairly good overall quality.

We checked out the workings. Psyche Revitalized, I guess. We networked.

There, we lingered on the steps.

I took another bowl of lace. 1857.

Cola had recently been re-discovered, and newly invented, this nineteenth century.

To the brand new era.

I still couldn't regain myself sometimes, despite.

She still huddled close to me. "Some days I'm glad we're alive," she says.

She hugged her head against my shoulder.

On days, she looked absolutely pretty. Her blonde hair was stunningly corn yellow.

We rode via modern transit line. The steam engine had been invented nearly six decades before.

Alexia and I stayed in a hotel. I kissed her on the back of the neck.

"How did you feel about the large serpent's cross?" She had been referring to the guild.
"I always felt they were better in the seventies," I said.
And that's the way she felt too.
Good thing she always made me feel intelligent.

We rummaged through books together, in the private library of Marseilles.
Art designs were posted on the wall.

Still, I always felt I could've been an excellent designer. Maybe, back when.

We had recently published a new book. A set of scrap notes

entitled, The New Phoenix Dealership Incorporated, in 1857, and 1859.

Contained were notes on travels, and hunting and hosting. Perfectly bound.

We were built on an astoundingly good plain. 1858-1859.

I watched her play the clarinet. Alexia had been a highly trained expert musician. And, eight other classic instruments, she knew very, very well, as well.

More: She also played light piano after that.

She had meant more to me, I said to her.
That she believed. I knew she knew me better.

And that held our third tour of France. The City of Lights looked radiant, back when, in 1682.

We'd stop for a croissant, and maybe a light pastry.

She still looked twenty-eight or twenty-six.
And she looked so pretty in her pink, pink, red and yellow outfit.

Later, it was 1860.

And more to that.
And more to that, in 1860-1861.

Alexia and I would spend the next decade elsewhere.

1861-1862. Following proper consultations in England and Italy, with our cadre and cadre forces, we decided to make a move again. To Austria, we settled.

The good lights went on for us, those years. They all shine for us, so very brightly so.

End of chapter.

25

THE 1860S-(???)

1864. Austria.

1866. We stayed in the cottage house.

I had hugged Alexia again. I had hugged her over and over.

We lounged on the long seat discussing our days, our dreams, our businesses, and what fueled the two of us. Her discussions smiled.

And she rejuvenated me, completely.

On some days I figured, I owed her that much.

For a while, we read poetry.

"Alexia?"
"Mmmm." She made a noise.

I snuggled closer to her on the long over seat.

"Did you ever feel bad about what happened?" she asked.
"Do you mean, do I feel bad?" I said to her.

"Mmm." She said again.
"Maybe," I said.

At some points, maybe. Maybe, I did.

"What's happens next?" she asked.

I took her out for a dinner. We had a nice steak, and some white cream sauce on it.

"There's too much action in these cities," I said to her.
When you're feeling good, and you're feeling up to it, I guess, she said.

Later we went out for some more strudel, together.

We lived in Austria briefly.

We had moved the base to Denmark, for a time.

Upon our return, we tested some very basic, again for a while. For those good moments, it felt like we were young again. She tested me.

She had hugged me, for over a minute or so.

Thank god, for her warmth.

We tried it out again. She had read more about the subject in some live Austrian style living book, with instructions. At some convention, she attended.

I kissed her once more.

Section ii.

1869. Copenhagen.

I also tried to make amends with Lady Victorian. I was reluctant, but I had promised to enchant her.

Always she wore white diamonds.
And in the new daytime, we'd start all over again. We would embrace tightly and very, very satisfyingly, over the span of only two nights.

And more. We continued.
We felt so good together. Me and Lady Victorian.

There we had been, generating more magic in the world.

And then, again and again, over and over, we discussed at length our futures in the world.

She'd kiss me, long, on the lips.

Section iii.

1872. We head back to America.

I took another tour. Maybe, probably, to collect some more of our income. Possibly, to buy up more land posts, I figured.

The apples are good and enjoyable, I say in German. Thanks.

26

THE 1870S

their version of a Western (1878), with Grey Fox; lightermann goes back to college

1878. Back in America. The Historical "Wild West".

Our adventure started at a inn. We had been staying at St. La Belle's.

I had attended with Grey Fox. He had worked his way through the main rooms.

Later we found out that Grey Fox was classified as a Navaho Apache. He had originated from close enough to Mexico.

We spent a week there.

After a week or so, they finally contacted me.

He, Penselton, basically hijacked me out of my dorm, and dragged me across the main room lobby.

What's the deal, I said.

Quiet, he said. You'll be absolutely quiet until we get there, he said. A larger man, a ruffian stood on the other end.

An attractive blonde woman, Ms. Hemingway, sat before me.

You've been contacted because you're the best. The note said that you were the best, she said to me.

She leaned forward to wipe the blood off the forehead and hair. He had hit me pretty hard, I guess.

I waited patiently. My dress shirt was untucked.

She was very thin, yet exceedingly voluptuous.

When we arrived, I found myself in a senator's office.

Senator Goodkind will be out to see you in a moment, she said.

Goodkind, I asked.

S*** up, said Penselton.

The large ruffian, stood close to the corner, eating from a plate-bowl of green grapes. His name turned out to be Lucasz.

When the Senator arrived, Penselton announced him.

We have this guy. We're not sure what to do with him, he said.

We'll keep him as he is, for now, and I'll give him the briefing in a few minutes or so, said Sen. Goodkind.

Apparently, explained:

A secret service solar earth energizer had been lifted from a government. Along with it, they, a band of cowboy terrorists had stolen, several documents, priceless artifacts, and paintings, and the Senator's highly esteemed, highly pretty daughter Nicole, and her cousin Lois. Also, at least four other very attractive good-looking women had been kidnapped, from very wealthy homes, and, rumors held, highly enslaved, on the enemy compound.

The cowboy ranch terrorists, led by the darkly sinister figure, Dutch; had sent several threat messages demanding strong political pull, and favors.

Senator Goodkind frowned.

He, and the government, needed someone to recover the stolen military equipment, from mysterious Secret Sacred Diablo Compound B, centered somewhere in mid-center of close-to Southern Nevada; and, recover the missing women, particularly, his daughter, the Senator worried. Also, important were the documents.

He had heard records that I had served as a military specialist, in my time, at a certain point. Also, the notes said that I was one of the best, and the best at the best, he reminded me.

Do you accept, he asked.

I'll accept for a quarter million, I thought.

And here's the team of seven specialists I assembled, to deal with the issue of finding Senator Goodkind's artifact treasures, and also his pretty daughter and the five other women that had been kidnapped.

(1) Me. Herkomar, the Best. I can speak over twenty-nine different languages. Also, I'm a genius swordsman, of incredible great skill. My motif: A white jacket outfit, and a red rose.

(2) Grey Fox. Werewolf-Changeling. Expert combat specialist, and field operative. In actuality, he can run over forty five miles per hour. When I asked him about that, he said, generally at least fifteen miles, is what he tells everyone. He doesn't like being challenged, he explained.

(3) "Happy Jack" John Davenport. Roundabout Gambler. All around good guy. Uses a whip. And a knife, if necessary. Expert at dealing with dynamite and dynamite fuse.

(4) Good Saint Jane. Female gunslinger. Carries a forty five revolver, with a rifle and a long weapons scope, as well. Thrilled to be a part of the mission. She always hits her target, she says.

(5) Percival the Third. Wears a (paladin) knight's outfit, complete with soldier's armor. Occasionally, he roams the streets as a highwayman. Records say he's saved the lives of at least two dozen women at one point. Speaks with a loud heroic voice tone.

(6) Jerome. Classic Book reader type. Also, he's an accountant.

And finally...

(7) Lightermann. Been to college at least three times. He looks like a blonde surfer type. Women think he's cute and very, very good-looking. Immortal. He can hold his breath under water for over two and a half minutes. Trying to save up money to pay his tuition from last year. Also, he uses dynamite too sometimes.

And that's the list. We assembled them in less than eight days.

Then we rode off through the canyons on horses.

I checked the documents files.
We took four large caravans with us, just in case.

Do we have the steady a plan for this one, asked Saint Jane.
Yeah, said Grey Fox.

Ours was to break in, delete a bunch of cowboy terrorists. Knock off as many as possible. Then Bring back the women, and the powerful earth energy weapon device.

"Sha-bot zae roe-daaaan..., bohn." said lightermann.

Very good, she thought.

Upon entrance to the area. We stashed the caravans.

Main Objective Number One: Break into the enemy compound.

What's all this about, asked the guy at the gate. Secret Diablo Compound B ran about a half a mile, by a third. A machine gun tower was held to the west side. The holders' row, held lightly to the east of that. Also, there was an armory, somewhere, probably in two spots, we figured.

Once we got into the machine gun tower, we knew we'd be fine. We had investigated the compound earlier.
Also, we needed to assassinate the main club terrorist.

We're here to see the man who operates this place, I said.

What business is this, he asked.

We bear good load, I said.
He paused.
I'll have to check it, he said.
Percival readied his long sword.

Grey Fox grabbed the watch guardsman. He had been hiding under a large canopy sheet, on a cart we carried with us.

He then made the were-wolf transformation. He punched the guard a few times, hard, in the head. Knocking him out, gone. Then he bent back the guy's shoulder, and tossed him.

Then he tore into a bunch of the other guardsman, who were hiding in the guardsmen's office, incapacitating them, and throwing some of them, at least fifty feet. Loudly, they screamed.

Percival had located one of the guards, and grabbed a set of keys. It had been in the middle of the night, slightly after two o'clock.

Happy Jack bit into a peach. It had been that simple.

Main Objective Number Two: Re-acquire the stolen earth energy weaponizer.

Clearly, we suspected this could be held in the weapon-smithing office

Maybe everyone in the compound was still sleeping.

We had Jerome act as an early scout, two days previous, to check on the locationing.

We had snuck him in, earlier, wearing a dress, and then also a cowboy outfit.

Later he explained to us, it was kept behind tight guard. It would take at least three men to bring it out of their held sector. I sent Grey Fox to take care of it.

Also, we needed to assure that the compound square was clear.

Dumm**s, I thought. That was why we needed to check the machine gun tower, which we captured easily.

I sent Happy Jack and Good Saint Jane, to pull a grab on that particular article.

They took a pistol apiece, and ascended the tower with them, after, Once, Grey Fox tore the door of the tower door down.

A few bullet shots went off. Also, a large stick of dynamite, maybe. But I'm glad they took care of it.

After four minutes, they made it to the top. Happy Jack waved his arm, in the moonlight, to signal. Good Saint Jane handled the machine gun, and blasted various troublesome riff raff, that were their way in the compound that late at night, to check on the noise. It was true. She never missed. Meanwhile, Grey Fox tore his way, fastly, through the compound squares, totally smashing up any compound terrorists that bothered to step in the light.

He entered the armory alone, but I knew he could handle it.

After a wait, various screams occurred.

Then, after a good twenty minutes, he managed from the building. He had hauled out the large energy weaponizer, and carried a bunch of roped paintings and some documents, in his arms, and slung over his back.

I had instructed him to take four of each, as proof that we'd been there.

And that was perfect. He could carry them all.

The energy weaponizer was huge, very metallic, and contraption-ey, made entirely of silver and brass beads. I was unsure if it would work at all, upon rescue of that item. However, regardless, as long as it was in our arms, and not in the arms of a cowboy terrorist; I felt the senator, and everyone else, would feel better about that.

Lightermann helped Grey Fox with some of the additionals, some documents and some highly expensive very pricey gold metallic artifacts, made of pure hard solid karats, warrior's plates, and silver and platinum, and red jewels.

Main Objective Number Three: Rescue the princesses.

The women had been held captive in the women's holders' building. Jerome reported to me, about this later. He explained in detail. I knew this situation might be concerning.

I decided to send Percival to pull the women out. He had captured, the keys, of course, in that time.

I sent him in alone, with his sword. That would be sufficient, I knew.

I felt a pang of worry. Would our caravans be enough to bring them all back with us?

Thirty minutes later. He emerged from the building with all thirty or so beautiful good-looking women. We took a count. There had been thirty-two women of them, in total, plus Percival. I made sure we had the two we needed though. The senator's daughter

Nicole, was accurately very slender and very pretty. She clung to Percival, and hugged him, nicely, in front of all of the other very good-looking women. Nicole's cousin, Lois, was cute too. She gave lightermann a nice little kiss later, I heard.

Very reassuring, I thought.

Happy Jack gave a wave. He brought up all fingers, five. And then he gave a big thumbs up.

Good Saint Jane was still in the watch tower, with the machine gun, blasting away, at miscellaneous cowboy terrorists.

And there was still that one last detail.

Main Objective Number Four: Eliminate the head main leader of the sinister cowboy terrorist gang.

His name had been Dutch.

Apparently, according to the Dossier report, Dutch Kelly, the terrorist leader, an Argentincan patriot, was known for wearing thin tight bandages wrapped around, his skull and arms, completely. He had been scarred due to an earlier incident with high explosives, year back. He wore nice expensively tailored dress clothes, and very dark black-tinted glasses too, it read.

Dutch, a former high league bullfighter, weapons soldier, and exterminator of peasants. He had gone too far, and had to be eliminated.

He was forty-one years old.

I confronted him myself, and I knew how to take care of it. He was staying in the second main building, which I entered, by myself.

I made my way through, careful not to get wet paint on my pure white jacket, with the red rose. The place was decorated very nicely, I thought.

When I had emerged from the building, I had assassinated the cowboy terrorist leader.

Are you ready, he had asked me. He had been sitting on a couch coating seat.
Then I punched him across the chest.

As mentioned, I had fought in the Hundred Years War, previous. I took a gold chalice with me, when I left.

Then we left what was the remains of the bullet-ridden compound Diablo B, devastated. Good riddance, we thought.

Grey Fox took the reins.
Fires had been set during that night too, reported Happy Jack.

Saint Jane nodded, appreciatively.
Jerome was busy reading a book, at the time.

We had finished our job, all seven of us, by four-thirty, in the morning.

And we rode at least four towns away, with the several several women, and the paintings, and the top secret energy earth device in the back.

"Yee-Haw!", said lightermann.

After we had ridden a little farther down the road, at a carrier square, I contacted Penselton, by telegraph.
He must've grunted about that, I figured.

He would have to send an additional two caravans, to aid in traveling the well-off princesses that we had rescued.

We rode back after that, well satisfied.

And, That was the story.

Afterwards, we celebrated.

Back at the office:
Ms. Hemingway wrote me a check for a hundred thousand.

Also, she gave me a good hug, too.

End of chapter.

27

THE 1880S

story about Pakistan; camera
invention, Herkomar meets another
woman, plus additional

A series of true stories.

Section i. demonstration of the camera.

This marvelous device, the modern photographer's camera,
was newly refashioned sometime during the 1860s. Involved was
the method of the inverted picture frame. Earlier, this was done by
tracing. Those days, during the 1880s and 1890s, it was completed

through development paper.

A lot of work, and specialized roomings went into these processes.

Earlier, we could rely on books, for storage on records, and memory. Then, Later, we could rely on photos, to tell the future and others.

I had purchased more than a few of these very modern devices for Alexia. She had been my girlfriend at that point and I loved her very much.

Section ii.

Now here's a separate story about lightermann. I was planning on putting this story in another chapter, but instead I'll put that story in this one.

Around 1880, or 1881. Lightermann decides to go back to college. We had shipped him off to the University of Naples, one of the original early colleges of Europe. So sad was he, to have to leave the states, for Europe again.

I spoke with him about this on numerous occasions. This was, actually, his third or fourth adventure through college again.

So lightermann, I asked him later. On my return, in 1883. What did you learn?
I learned much, he said. Very interesting platforms, he said.

Probably he had been focusing on the good looking young women of Naples, I figured.

Lightermann, how do you expect me to pay for all this? These journeyings and gallivantings all over and throughout the countries.

I had known that he could pay for all this himself, however, I just wanted to point out to him, that he was spending off our dime, of the new re-fashioned Trinity , later to call ourselves, Team Five, which I think I mentioned in an earlier chapter. How important, we were.

Um, said lightermann.

Fine, I said. Just think about that, I said. And We paid his expense bill anyway.

Next section.
Section iii.

Story about Pakistan. 1940. This is important. Another noted issuance occurred across the country maybe sixty or eighty years after. It was entitled Lahore. That was the story of Pakistan, and the creation of a new independent state. There was a level of demand for a second city, close to India. Some had no idea how relevant this was. Later on, this country would become crucially important, in the early mid-twenty first century, for a reason dealing with openings of new and greater technology. Through that, it became about saving the world.

There they proved their worth, in the twenty-first century, we had realized

I had to include this section, mind you. For marvelous tech reasons. If some don't know why that is, I probably won't explain right here. Trust me, this new country was important. I knew. I knew even then.

Section iv.

1876. And, again, I met a very good-looking woman, from America, in the 1860s.

Her name was D****. D**** Buchanan. She looked around twenty-five.

"How acclaims," I asked.
"To the very good thought of that," she said.

She was, of course, very pretty. And she had an intelligent mind. That said, we felt like royalty.

Also: Moreover, We had closed another major land deal that year.

I'll have her, to thank for it, I suppose.

Section v.

1885. I called up Alexia. She had been staying in Austria, for that season.

Alexia, how would you like to make it to the party? I asked.
Hon, I'm very sort of busy in league this month. Maybe I'll make it next year, she said.

That's fine, I'm sorry, I thought. And then I arranged for another meeting with a lab assistant.

There was another story about Alexia, which became very relevant years later.

Section vi.

Back forward:

1889. For a while, I felt over-worked.

I flipped through a trade journal.

There was another article on drug-meal.

I took another light hit of cigarette. We shared a bowl of lace together.
Cooking powder had become used frequently, and more often, that century. For a while, it seemed the substance was available anywhere.

They had printed articles on imperviousness, was the notion.

I attended another wedding for someone at some point afterwards. The woman's name had been Trish.
She was apparently another American.

O' What a thrilling ceremonial tradition, this had turned out to be. I rejoiced, with the rest of them, and then attended, the glorious union again, at another follow-up party.

Section vi., continued.

A girl threw some pretty flowers.

A close female friend of mine, Christiana, had, of course been invited, as well. We re-acquainted as a duo.
I held her closely.

For a while, this held me, great. And a very good time was had by all.

Thank you.
-Herkomar

End of chapter.

28

THE LATER 1880S

discovery of Eiko, he proposes theory of immortality

1888. America. Then Kyoto.

There was a call for me to make a visit to Japan. Someone had published an important article work. Apparently he hailed from Kyoto, originally. His name had been Eiko.

I had heard of his work and studies.

It was a long trip, and an important voyage, and we had mapped it out.

So there, I was in line, with a booked meeting with him.

I was greeted at the door, a cute, pretty dark-haired girl. Apparently, this was his great niece (Ley Hanza). I asked Ley Hanza, when he'd be available to speak with me. She scheduled me close to a month after.

I stayed in Kyoto, for over two months.
It had been very pleasant living.

Eiko's article, published in New Science and Gazette, had concerned the principles of scientific immortality, and great history of achievement.

He had broadcast several points in the article, relating to proper nutrition, and good worldly value.

Asserted:
One, Good health, provides for natural wisdom and strength. -eiko-
Two, Immortality, and, is, ordained to those of good aptitude, and very affirmable, at.las, crucially exceptional, strong life-living. And, Three, also, must word append, that proper isles, must be held. And, there, they, -furthermore- station correctly. -eiko.

And more like that.

There were many other points of interest, throughout the article.
On immortality, I realized; the consumer guidebook had noted him to be a leading world expert, on the subject.

I spoke with him about this later. He had been slightly over seventy eight years at the time. He, operatively, seemed to be only twenty two years old, in terms of appearance. A gifted magician, and a scientist. He was handsome, with very sharply defined good-looks, and very quick. He could walk four times faster, than at least most individuals could run.

He was known to be the inventor of basically anything.

Born to a stunning noble family, of samurai background; This had been in 1809, I assumed. He himself had fought in over three wars, and was mainly used as a combat field reporter.

He was to have written for several princely journals. By that, they had managed to defeat Russia.

Useful reports, they had claimed.

Hanna would have liked this fellow, I guess.

He was, as mentioned, by several in company, a startlingly brilliant individual.

He dyed his hair pure white, some might've suspected. However, I later learned, that was his hair's natural light color When he hit the year 1823, it bleached over, by itself.)

Also:
Eiko Eiko had been married twice, divorced once, and widowed

later. His first wife divorced him over a matter concerning his perpetual sharpened youthfulness. Lightly irritated, she was about the subject; that she would age lightly, and he would always be assumed to be a very good-looking twenty-two. Later, she re-married, to, ironically enough, a younger thirty-something male, anyway.

His second wife was a gorgeous female model. She had apparently expired herself, due to grief, after Eiko had left the country in 1856, when he was writing a field report, on activities in New Dublin. Four years after, he had left her alone. After the third year, she was gone.

He went on to continue his several works.

So there I was in Kyoto.

"Eiko. Let me ask you this. Why are we here?"
"Why are we here?" he asked.
"Why do immortals exist? What is, um, the scientific reasoning behind the existence of immortals?" I said, re-phrasing my earlier question.
His response: "We're born geniuses," he explained.

Eiko's articles went to prove, certain incredible super genius brains, are capable of producing brain chemicals, that can well rejuvenate skin, and keep appearances, enhanced, and immortally prime-looking.

We look faster, and we heal faster, he noted. Most of us, are stronger, indeed.

Geniuses become more and more intelligent every day, is known, by geniuses.

Eiko was a super genius, and I was a super genius (I could speak over thirty-five different languages, and I have near perfect calculatory skills, as he could).

This seemed to concur, with my own evidence. Basically, everyone who had been on my team, was, and is, a total genius. With maybe the exception of Grey Fox, who, of course, was bitten by a master wolf, to ordain his powers of immortality; my whole team were all super geniuses besides.

Quite a extraordinary notion, I realized.

What's the chance of that skill, man?

They say at least one immortal is born close to the beginning of every century, he, Eiko, had stated.

And after that, we had adopted the name Team Five.

Seeing that, there were five of us.

We had made Eiko a large offer, with a very high cash long-term dealer contract.

All and all, It had been a great stay in Kyoto. I had stayed for four months later. The world was known to be very pleasant and good-looking.

Section ii.

1889. Wednesday. In August.

Rumors had it that there were more flying experiments being conducted, that year.

Someone, by the name of J. Hawkes, had invented another early helicopter machine. With an early jet boost and jumper system, Apparently, it operated full on steam.

I was able to watch this early flight engine module, in effect, six months later, in 1891.

In America.

1892. Friday. In November.

There. That had been a good invitation, as well.

And all was truly great and marvelous.

I had purchased a new company, one that primarily dealt in high level heavy security equipment (and technology).

Aces Management Supplies, they said. Exceeding, was our firm. Gorgeous, were the femmes.

To new accomplishments, we suggested.

And, Cheers.

1893.

End of chapter.

29

THE 1890S

read <u>the time machine</u>, studies in time travel, with I Victorian

1896. I had purchased a book by H.G. Wells, that year. My curiosity was peaked. The book entitled The Time Machine. Apparently, there had been a major success.

Through the breakthrough, I figured, certain good tasks would be possible.

I consulted my roster. Eiko would know about something like this.

I invited him to a meeting.

1898. Denmark.

"Eiko?" I said at the doorpost.
"Yes," he asked.
"Can we do something like this?" I said. I showed him a copy of the H. G. Wells time travel book.
He looked it over a moment.
"This is just a book," he said. Sort of like a commercial, he tried to explain.
"Fine. Fine." No luck there, I guess.

I had to go straight to the source then.

1898. England.

I asked Lady Victorian to help me out. She still looked heavenly great.
She looked through the book that I presented to her.

She laughed, and then clucked her tongue, a bit.

"Herkomar," she said: "I want to crack up about this. Because you read this in a book, you think it's possible?"
"I had intended, that it is possible. It's written right there on the page." I said, firmly.
Victorian paused to herself. She couldn't help but smirk a bit.
For a long moment, she seemed more slightly well oriented, and very highly sophisticated-looking, and exceedingly more attractive.
"Yes," she said, calmly.
"If it says, 'science', it means, we can do it, right?" I mentioned.
She smiled, very pleasantly.

"Incidentally, and ironically, I actually might have access to the gadget, that might meet your needs," she finally admitted, very serious.

Interesting, I thought. Interesting, as well. I knew she had been holding out on me.

She opened the door more completely.

Apparently, Lady Victorian had befriended a stage magician, years past, in around 1852. After that magician, Hanni-Moss, had passed away, he had left a remainder to those who fully supported his work. Lady Victorian had inherited a good major sum, and she obtained certain prized artifacts from his show vault.

He had apparently left her a magician's device that might've worked, for me, to get the results I needed. In terms of time travel, she had mentioned.

"Did you have interest with him?" I asked her.
"No, but I did present him a good mind, sort of," she explained.
"Oh, I gotcha," I said.

"Let's go to lunch, Herkomar," she said.

We went out for an early lunch, that day.
It was an even day during the autumn.

"What's this for?" she asked.

"I merely wanted to look up some tables. It's important to establish..."

"To establish what?" she said.

"To establish, for us, once again, that we're at a higher technological wave of achievement..."

"At time machining?" she asked.

"I agree. Of course. I was speaking of proper movement..."

"That's fine," she interrupted, and considered. "Uh huh. Then, yes, as requested, I said it. I might have a wizard's machine that can service that angle," she included. Thoughtfully.

The Story and Legend of Hanni-Moss the Great.

Found, as an adult magic wizard, at the young age of eighteen, Hanni-Moss began his brilliant career service, performing magic feats with his dazzling array of assistants, directly on stage.

This was the way that Lady Victorian told the story:

Most often, it seemed, he was known for the disappearing glasses trick. He'd stand in, on stage with a podium before him, and give the announcements. A curtain concealed the front, of a tower pyramid of stacked wine glasses filled with red water, with a large painting of a rose, in front of it. He was known to do the same with a yacht. The boat ran about eight to eighteen feet long. He called the order. Someone else, standing close to the left, would draw the string and the curtain would fall, to reveal the wine glasses, and yacht, and the painting, had vanished.

Also, In addition, Hanni-Moss had a situation involving alcohol. One day, he went home, and drank too much. For a performance, he could not fight enough. And then he stumbled. And that was the last, they ever saw of him.

He had built several contraptions, throughout his life, and to aid him, including a time tunnel, which he claimed, he found to work, himself.

But not to his desired results, which was reported by someone else.

1898.

We took a long pause.

I checked the log scenery for a moment.

section ii.

Victorian took me up to his, her magician friend's, old apartment studio flat. She had the keys already.

Numerous magician's devices were scattered throughout, wood boxes, large crosses, crystal glass implements, and sharp cutting devices, strong-looking chains, and a panel of sharp magician's swords, and other apparatuses. Within the second room, held the time tunnel, she explained.

"Is this it?" I asked.

"Aye," she said.

It had been a major contraption, I noted.

A large wooden box of oak, with a long medium dark blue piece of cloth, hanging, curtains-style over the entrance of the box, at the front.

"Well, go on," she said. "Aren't you going to try out the Time Tunnel?" she asked.

I thought a bit to myself.

"You're not scared, are you?" she asked.

She lit a cigarette. They had re-developed cola again at some point, that century.

"Have you ever tried this machine out yourself, Vi?" I asked.

"Not really," she said.

"Let me see if this works," I said.

And then I entered, through the long blue curtain sheet.

Cool inside, I thought.

Once inside,

I found myself struggling to get through a bunch of hanging sheets, which were heavy. In very dim light, I worked my way through the tunnel.

To the end, opposing my entrance was, a long white hallway. Filled, the hallway, rows and rows of clocks (a wide-range assortment). Tables, with clocks on them. Wood shelves, with clocks on them.

A pendulum clock was held at the other end.

Loud ticking occurred, Tick tick tick.

Tick tick tick, came an answer, slightly femininely.

Perplexed, I was for a moment.

I surveyed the scene a bit, then picked up a small working blue alarm clock. I held it to my ear for a moment, to hear the ticking.

Rome.
84. B.C.E.

I found myself surrounded by an army of Gladiators, in a tight large arena. I picked up a large heavy sword from a fallen body, and took a swing.

I had made one of my targets, on the leg. A snarling eight foot tall gladiator, let out a scream.
He grabbed the hit of the sword, and growled, then broke part of the blade.

Several of the other gladiators took notice. They had me scanned me, and my presence.

I held on to the remainder of my broken weapon, and looked around a bit, to indicate I might not have been there, in actuality, fully, or maybe there were something more interesting, in the arena, on which to focus.

However, they had decided, collectively, that they did not really care for any of my shenanigans. Clearly, I was a newcomer, they noticed. They had preferably wanted to stomp me, it seemed.

Yeaaargh, a few of them screamed.

So I ran.

And I ran.

To one of the entrances to the large arena, or, coliseum, I guess. I struggled to pull forth the door.

At least eight other large muscled gladiators slowly charged in my direction.

And it seems, I managed to pull the door just in time. Open, I ran through.

Egypt. 288 B.C.E.

And there I was, surrounded in a harem. I closed the door behind me.

In the gorgeous light sanctuary, in the top of an early early office pyramid-castle, I guessed.

The light of the gorgeous sun leaked in through a gap in the wall.

I dropped the broken weapon from Ancient Rome, to the hard stone flooring.

There I waited.

A pool of cold cool water was there.
And, four very beautiful girls, held there. They were, all four, gorgeously postured.

One had gorgeous bronze skin. Another was the color of peach. A third, was gorgeously white-skinned. A fourth was a tall tanned blonde vixen.

They approached me, slowly, with their good looking outfits, neatly pressed. Their presence comforted me.

The four beautiful women had surrounded. And then they put me at gorgeous modern peace of high tranquility. I stayed there for at least eight hours, and discussed abstracts. They seemed very enlightened and intelligent.

We stayed there for another additional two hours longer, afterwards.

1898. Back in England. A European studio flat.

"Herkomar?"

The other end of the time tunnel led out into a third or fourth room of the apartment, back in London. Once you get through the time tunnel, you come out the other side, she explained.

Lady Victorian tried waking me up. And there I was.

"Herkomar?" she said.
"Yeah," I said, slightly gruff.

"Did it work?" she asked.
"Give me a moment," I said. "I need to check on something," I said.

I brought myself up. Then I checked outside.

I needed a bit of fresh air. I went out into the street. I stood in the middle, and studied the building for a moment.

Lady Vi followed me outside.

"Did it work?" she asked again.
"Yes," I said.
She paused.
"Yes, then," she said.

And.
Then,
"We'll still have to try the machine 'The time studio machine' once more again," I pointed out to her.

Four months later.

We gathered lightermann. We brought with us many packs.

The three of us were to try the Time Tunnel, as a group.

Together we entered.
The large white hallway with the clocks, ticked away.
"Are you ready?"
Lady Victorian; she nodded.
I moment-selected a good one.
"Awesome," said lightermann.
And all three of us placed our hands on the clock.

Tick, tick tick tick, came a voice.

And, in a moment, together, we were transported away; and to other great destination(s).

End of chapter.

30

220 B.C.(???)

Victoria and Herkomar in Ancient Rome

220 B.C.E. We awoke in a field somewhere close to Rome, I felt. Or guessed. I was vaguely unsure.

"Where's lightermann?" she, Lady Victorian, asked.
"One moment.... Let me just gather," I said.
"What happened to lightermann?" she said again.
"I'm not sure," I finally responded.

I gathered the pack we had taken with us. We took a quick meal.

We walked to a nearby stable house, with our food and provisions.
She lit a gold cigarette, for herself.

"Again, what was the point of this?" she griped.
"I was hoping to find Constiglione." Was my answer, meek.
"Well, that's just great," she said. "And now we have to find

lightermann too," she pointed out, astutely, I suppose.

I knocked on the door. It had been answered by a bright nice-looking fellow, clearly a farmer, in his early twenties.

"We're traveling along the road," I said, in early latin, very, very early form of Italian. I knew the language, basically. I was fairly certain that was correct.

The guy's name was Rhawn.

I introduced myself as Odysseus. There with my female traveling companion, I. Victorian, who I introduced as the gorgeous Vivien Delaney.

He greeted us, and let us in for a moment. I handed him, some very modern day coin of thirty-five cent, by which he Rhawn, was actually very impressed.

"We're Irishyre," I explained.

And he nodded.

"We're actually from the Late Industrial science future. We were sent from England, Germany, Hungary, and America," she mentioned to him later.

He frowned.

"I don't know why he makes that stuff up," she said, in English.

This slightly perplexed Rhawn. He probably didn't speak much of her native language at all.

I don't know why I bring this up. I actually suspected that, with a time machine, in order, we would be able to track down Constiglione.

Later, when experimenting with the time tunnel machine, I could travel back in time, but I couldn't pinpoint the locations exactly. Even if we wound up in a destination, in which Constiglione was still alive, then I still wouldn't know where to find him.

Also, some of the destination year gates, I guess worked sort of randomly.

Quite often I missed my dear associate, Constiglione. Quite often now, I had often missed lightermann, as well.

"Maybe we should've left lightermann behind, in the future," I suggested.

With that, she punched me in the neck.

And yet we had a good meal, while we were there. I had grabbed a few plates, which I had purchased from him.

Section ii.

Next, We took a visit to see the local royalty. And procure some artifacts, so that we might explain better.

We had to worry at some points, I guess.

However, there was still a meeting post.

"To prove it works," was my explanation.

Her name was Freyja, and she was very, very pretty, with good-looking blue eyes, and she was only sixteen years old, at the time, and very slender.

We had paid for a banquet for her, including large fried meats, and lamb or beef steak.

We re-introduced ourselves. This time, I as Herkomar. And, of course, with the good lady Delaney

"How dy'doe, Herk-o-mar," Freyja said. She was attempting to imitate my accent.

Lady Victorian became angry and embarrassed.

I brought them several gifts. One, a finely crafted string instrument. Two, a nice noble light blue comfort (lt. comfort) scarf-wrap, that someone else had woven. I had kept it with me, and then to present to her as a gift.

At a certain point, we had showed her how to dance.

I had purchased a rhythm maker, from her older cousin, Lo'thor.

The party and I still had shared some truly outstandingly great evenings together.

Later, we enjoyed another great feast, complete, with all the choice meats, and cold beverages.

And the very next day, we partied again.

It came to a point, another one of Freyja's cousins, Bluumeade, wanted to fight with me.

He hit me over the head with a club.

That was a slight altercation, which I learned to step past that one, based on good moral principles.

That was what happened.

We stayed there, at the royals' luxury coliseum house, for two or more weeks, before the time tunnel transported us elsewhere.

End of chapter.

31

880 B.C.(???)

Victoria and Herkomar in
Ancient Mesopotamia

To 880 B.C.E.
Ancient Sumeria, maybe.

We took a break where we stayed, in ancient Sumeria. Lady Vi.
was still very angry.

There was a good spring of cold water. We lounged for a bit
around the cool water zone, by an oasis, by the river.

"Isn't this place great?" I asked.
"Why would you think I'd enjoy this," she said.

I myself found it all interesting quality. But that was me, and quite often, I am a perpetual optimist.

Lady Vi merely wanted to go back to the future. Perhaps, she missed her dear friends.

I still missed Constiglione, is what I thought.

My associates I loved, I knew. I had wanted to share a voyage with my good associates, as mentioned.

Why would this be an issue? I wondered.

And, Mid-Early in the morning:

We took a tour of the table market in Mesopotamia. Mesopotamia, I noticed, I guess that was correct. I was sure that would pick up her spirits, but it didn't. She didn't care.
She wanted to go home.

Good-looking women are very fragile, I realize.

We rented a pair of dromedaries.

She lit another cigarette.

We took a long break to examine the weather. Quite a good bit of sun for the first six hours or so. Then, some darker clouds began to build over the next few days. We had been expecting dry weather, but, instead, the weather became largely moist and wet.

I pondered the meaning of this. Then I shifted -'shivered'- a bit.

Very lightly, we worried.

Lady Victorian started to cry.

We took shelter by an inn cathedral. An inn cathedral?- she asked.

And, then, thankfully, after four and a half days, we time voyaged back to our original time spot, of the later 1898. I knew, based on earlier experience, the time tunnel would surely take us back to our original point of departure.

We awoke at the end of the chamber, in full garbs. Some of the artifacts that we'd taken with ours, didn't transfer well.

The artifacts that I left, for property of Romans, I found again in my pack. The food provisions were still gone, of course, for we had eaten most of them.

We found out later, that sometimes when metal items are brought to the future, they don't preserve. I had nabbed a nice strong power sword, from ancient Sumeria, which didn't quite make the future transfer. When I brought it into forward, it had rusted, and was considered partially unusable. A shame, it had been a nice artifact. I intended on bringing it back as a gift for a friend of mine, however, at that point I would have to buy him something else.

I apologized profusely to Lady Vi., afterwards. She gave me a big hug, and said she was sorry.

"I love you, Herkomar," she said. I held her in my arms.

We had dinner together again, that night.

The Big Six included drugs, as well.-Herk

As for lightermann, well, that's another story which I'll probably tell later.

End of chapter.

32

2612A.D.

lightermann teleports to the future

I received the story from lightermann somewhere around the year 1904.

Apparently, the time tunnel had teleported him to the future. The year had been estimated to 2612. He had been brought somewhere around Portugal, or Spain. This was where he stayed for close to fourteen months. I worried about that, that he mentioned that.

For a while, he had taken to wandering the future streets of Portugal, or future Spain maybe, for close to two and a half weeks, until he had been adopted by an adult family of four, which consisted of a matron, Heidi, and three other young adult females.

Together, they lived, over the next three and a half months.

The unit spoke a vague futurized form of English, as well. However their language, was so modern, he was barely able to discern it.

After a while, lightermann had merely trained them.

"I am lightermann. I am a visitor of the time tunnel technologies, from the past, of the very late beautiful 19th century. England or Sweden. I am a wandering immortal," he said and announced.

"Yes, lightermann," Tatiana, and Claire said. "Yes, lightermann," he had trained them to say, in conversation, after each time he spoke, when detected to be a comment, or after each request, from lightermann.

One of the girls, Shyy was twenty-six, and still in college, and pursuing a series of degrees. He had taught her vague symbols of mathematics, and important historical foundations, that he had remembered.

"Yes, lightermann," she said obediently. "Yes, lightermann, indeed," she said.

Shyy gave him a little kiss, he told me.

The food there had been the works of highly graded technology. Lightermann would not comment over whether it was good or bad. Mostly, it consisted of synthesized versions of beef-pork.

He had tried out their food dispenser, quite a bit. It seemed basically unlimited, he noted.

Quite often, he would try the synthesized beef-pork, wrapped in freshly synthesized flour tortillas.

They did not require lightermann to procure an occupation. There was no need to. The world of future Portugal (or future Spain? Maybe), seemed highly utopian. Virtually unlimited, was the economy.

They had several other bits. Watcher technology, he mentioned. Cameras had become more evolved, and compactized. Information and data was all storable on compact, pocket devices.

He had also described a later version of the television set, complete with holographic video. Video?, we asked. Had he been serious. That sounds *way* cool. He tried some of the sets out himself. To his grading, it worked well. It created the illusion of being elsewhere. There were holiday sites, on tiny disc sets, including Future Rome, Future Paris, and Future Tokyo. Future America discs, also sold very, very well. He had taken the tour of future Alabama, at least ten or twenty times, in a row.

Also, he said, Herkomar was proven correct about those investments. He was very smart to buy up, said lightermann.

Thank you, I noted.

Future music, he described, as reminiscent of vaguely classical, to his memory. I'm glad he recalled that, I thought.

Quite often, it seemed based on more on fashioned, basic

computer-derived memory rhythms, he said. Computers? Asks the reader. I'll explain later. –Herk

It all sounded a bit to him like a future version of Friedrich Chopin.

Quite often, the music relaxed him.

He saw a version of a future play, or opera, in fact, as well, he mentioned to me later. One of the young women with whom he was staying, Shyy, actually, had taken him out for a night on the town.

It seemed to what was called, a high motion action play. The future theatre was engrossingly major. The several voice intonations were strong and potent.

The characters moved slowly, then quickly, then quicker, and often used highly interesting acrobatic arm and hand and acrobatic leg simulations.

There was even a light show movement, afterwards, he described.

That was fine too, he said. Everything was future.

I listened.

He also changed the subject to future *druegas*.

They had druegas of high future excellence, he proudly reported.

Apparently, he toured the future version of a coke den.

Obviously it was much cleaner, he mentioned to me. The *drue-gas* were of high excellence, he reminded. Taken as powdered form, lightning powder accelerated brain activity, agility, and speed ability. Also, there was an edible chewing nugget available, called 'Olavv nuggets', that totally muscle enhanced the body, very, very good, and increased intelligences dramatically. Also, certain types of the chewing nugget cured, of any ailment.

He had one in a biscuit sandwich. It tasted pretty good, in fact, he said later.

Also, all the women in the entire country, he described of his visit to the future, were all very well fashionable. This seemed like very good news to me, I thought.

◇━━━◆━━━◇

Wow, I said to him. Our dear precious lightermann. Still he looks nineteen or twenty. Thank you for enlightening us with the story of your tour of future Spain or Europe, I mentioned to him.

Truly, was a great thought.
Lady Victorian gave him a light kiss, upon his return, at the end.

Thanks.

◇━━━◆━━━◇

End of chapter.

◇━━━◆━━━◇

PART V

The Golden Age
(late Industrial)

The Golden Age (late Industrial)

1920s-studies in flight, Herkomar has a daughter (intro)

1930s-brief interlude with john spade.

1940s-Have to rescue Grey Fox, from American Military Studies Base

1950s-read <u>Chronicles of Superman</u>, female character (and lightermann) wants to be Superhero

1960s and 1970s-build rocket; Victorian and Grey Fox become involved with peace movement

1980s and 1990s-funeral for an co-worker friend, and then, the 1990s; parody of a Christmas carol

33

THE 1920S

studies in flight, Herkomar
has a daughter (intro)

A chapter in three basic sections.

Section i.

1914. Copenhagen. Ten years after invention of the airplane, we decided to conduct our own studies in flight.

I had Eiko work on a design.

He went through schema after schema.

After twenty three designs, we finally selected, and approved one. One particular design was apparently our favorite.

He spent a month working on the construction. Made of sleek aerodynamic designer metal, the complete product was devised as a pure carrier of quick and modern dimension and high speed dynamic.

Eiko's fast jet design flew like a beauty. Piloted, it had to be flown manually. We hired a local field hand and his wife, Heidi, to take the test ride.

The jet plane flew at over eighty miles per hour, we clocked. And it reached heights exceeding two miles, we tested and estimated.

We stood on the range, sipping cool iced tea, and happy with our achievement.

We applauded at our great success.

I stood there with two attractive young lady friends, Cara and Stacy. I wondered, how long that one would last.

We stood back a moment, over our general accomplishment.

And close to a week or a year after, a famous German scientist published his General Theory of Relativity.

Section ii.

1919. Back in America.

We sat at the ranch, reading newspapers.

"Grey Fox, can you grow wings?" I asked him.

He thought for a moment.
"Maybe," he suggested.
"How long will it take?"
"A week or so, maybe?" he guessed.
"Can you try for me?" I asked.
"Sure. Maybe. Hold up. Give me a moment."

He left the room for a half an hour. When he returned, he came back a large set of gorgeous, fourteen-foot long, white and lt. blue leather wings growing out of his back.

"Like this?" he said.
"That is awesome," I commented.
"Great," he said. "Whatever," he said.
"Can we test them?" I asked.
"Test them?" he asked.
"I just want to see if you can fly."
"Not right now...," he said.... "In fact, no," he said after giving it some more thought.

"Fine by me," I said, then.
And he went back to reading his newspaper.

Section iii.

Another story. 1926. Amsterdam.

It was around this time, Alexia had a surprise, for me. She wanted to introduce me to someone new.
The girl had red-brown hair, she wore a red blouse. A smart

figure on her, I noticed. She appeared around eighteen or nineteen years old.

"Who is this aching beauty?" I asked Alexia.
"That happens to be your daughter, hon. So don't get excited," she told me.

The young woman's name was Donna Herkomar. And she was thirty-two years old. Height-wise, she was five foot nine, or five eleven or five twelve, in correct footwear.

A few things I have to mention. Alexia was never a member of Team Five. She was seen as a private independent acquaintance and consultant of my own. For a while, Alexia went to law school.

Our daughter was, of course, born sometime around the summer of eighteen ninety-two.

I took them out for a good meal. Donna, back when, seemed slightly gripey. She had been dating an Italian physicist, I later learned. Slightly proud, I thought.

I paid for the meal, and then I took off.

"How do I know she's my daughter?" I asked Alexia, in private.
"Of course, she's your daughter, Herkomar. Look how intelligent she looks," Was the answer.

I thought about that logic for a moment. Surely, it made definitive sense to Alexia.

1928. Two years later. England. I had been working late with a trade union those days.

After midnight, I received a phone-call.
Half asleep, I crawled out of bed and answered the phone.

"Herkomar," I said.
"Herkomar?"
"Yeh, what do you want?"
"It's me, it's Donna," she said.
"Donna? I don't know any Donna's," I said.
"Herkomar, it's me. It's your daughter, Donna Herkomar."
I paused, momentarily embarrassed. "Aw, jeepe, I'm sorry, that's right....," I said.
"Dad, I need to talk to you. We met two years ago."
"...that's right...that's right...hon, it's after three o'clock in the morning here..."
"Dad...Dad...it's different here, Herkomar." I was surprised, she called me 'Dad'.
"...fine, I guess...we can talk....what's going on..."
"I want to talk to you in private," she said.
"No, we can talk here," I said.
"Fine, fine, Herkomar," she said.
"Great, hon. That's great."
She paused.
"I need a job, Dad," she said.
"...sure...sure...that's no problem..."
"I want to work for your operatives, Dad,"
"fine...fine...we'll plug you in, somewhere, if you want...."
"I love you, Daddy," she said.

"No problem," I said.
She paused again.
"So how's your mother, by the way?" I asked her.

We talked a bit, and then I arranged for her to make an appointment with me.

I spoke with her mother, a few days after that. Apparently, our daughter had recently lost her previous job as a waitress at a food service restaurant.

I was more than happy to help her out.

We gave Donna intern status for our production company, out west.

For good work, I offered her a reasonable stipend. Mostly I took the days off, while she did her work in our booking department.
The crew found her very efficient, smart and upward-seeking.

Brilliant and ecstatic, I was to take care of her.
I purchased some research materials for her to work through. For a while later, she procured her own apartment spaces.

On the days, she'd attend high fashion meetings.
On the weekends, she'd pilot more sailings.

My daughter was highly connected to three or eight genius

societies, including some very prestigious operations.

Moreover.

Donna lived in America for that time. April 1926, and May-August 1928, until far later.

And more.

Section iv.

December 1928. England.

Me with Eva.

I gave her a light kiss on the cheek, as she slept in bed. She purred, softly, womanly.

Warm, she felt.

I fixed myself a glass of water, and a cold hard sandwich.

How I loved you, Alexia.

And that was that.

End chapter.

Also:

34

THE 1930S

Bonus scene with John Spade.

An un-related quick anecdote...
The re-introduction of Spade.

1937. St. Patrick's Day Festival. Anaheim. West Virginia.

I found him once again, at an open tavern, somewhere later in that decade. My girlfriend and I had been nesting at a small town apartment. He still looked to be around thirty-eight years old.

"Hey, it's been a while since I've seen you, around here...," I said. He looked off at me, slightly. "Buzz off," he said, rudely.

Then he finished his drink, good old-fashioned American, and he left.

And, That was the last, I saw of him, for those four or six decades.

And that's the story.

End Interlude.

The story is that John Spade had been a practical journalist, a traveler and an archivist. He had worked for part time hours at the Iowa Dailies set, and spent his free time as a vague freedom fighter for the Jermanian News Network, column or circuit, or order.

Upon my re-encounter with him I wondered, had time been that long? Had there been that many centuries since we'd last met? There had been a report of a light earthquake in San Francisco, which he was closer to field, those days. By the 1940s, he seemed a slightly weathered veteran columnist. The moral of the story, if you don't have time for someone then, they might not make time to speak with you later, I guess.

And that was the story of that, for an American hero.

The 1950s had always been a more pragmatic decade, in which we well honored, and were well regarded, and ordered and discussed our championships. Achievement became an article of substance, so to say it. Time had taken a closer effect, and we saw new and bright wall and bill board, and of that motif which were diamond wrist watches and color printing and cold brand sodas, of course, to which we commodified and purchased, for to enjoy and whet our appetites.

That to ours, was our building of utopian thought and matter, and initiative.

Bonus, Interlude, II:

Article on Will Cunningham, which is included for text reasons:

1961.

One of the pretty blonde secretaries bought Will Cunningham a nice red sweater. Will loved that sweater. He wore the sweater quite often, and it pleased her. One day, he accidentally spilled ink on the sweater. Oh no, he thought. So he stopped wearing it to the office. He didn't want the secretary to know.

But one day, she asked. Why don't you wear that sweater I bought for you, she asked him.

He started to cry. He then confessed to her that he had spilled ink on the sweater.

That's okay, she said. I bought the sweater to keep you warm.

So Will Cunningham wore the sweater anyway, and it kept him warm during the winter.

And that's the story.

35

THE 1940S

Have to rescue Grey Fox, from North American Military Studies Base

Operation: MOLTOR ROCK.

There were stories behind Grey Fox. There existed, rumors of capture.

Every time someone caught him as a werewolf, he told me, all he'd have to do, is lay low for two decades or so, and the newspapers would be convinced that the wolfen stories were all a bunch of hoaxes.

There were other points, of course, as mentioned.

One morning, in Autumn, I received a phone call. We had been staying in America for the decade, in the late 1940s. It was 1948, that year.

"Hello?" I asked.
"Herkomar, it's me."
I recognized the voice. It belonged to Grey Fox.
"Oh, that's great. How's coming?" I asked.
"Herk, I'm in troub**."
"What?" I asked.
"Need you to come by. I'm in New Mexico," he said.
"What?" I asked again.
And then he hung up.

He called up half a minute after that. And then he explained. Grey Fox had been captured by a North American Military Studies Base. Two years previous, I had sent him across to Europe, and later Romania. Upon his return to the U.S., there had been a brawl, in country, somewhere in New Mexico, at a military roadside tavern, and the military police had caught him, and tranquilized him, in midst of a werewolf transformation. They had allowed him one phone call, basically.

I had earlier escapades with Grey Fox, in which we were sent to rescue someone else together. At that point, the rest of the gang and I would have to rescue Grey Fox.

"Place General Thomas Collins on the guest list," I instructed him. "What for," he said. "Just do it," I told him.

And then I decided to round up the good team.

Lightermann had been staying in Reykjavik those days. No luck there, right.

Lady Victorian was staying close to Florida. I contacted her.

Also, Eiko was working on a plant close to Utah. I placed a call to him, as well.

There was a flight to New Mexico.

And, of course, we went in proper gear.

I was, of course, of light German nationality, so I disguised my origin, with an U.S. American General outfit, four and a half stars, of course, who I accurately represented. I wiped the dust off, and put on my contact uniform. I straightened up. I was to represent America.

Lady Victorian, a Brit, had placed herself in the uniform of a visiting female Russian, a three star general.

We introduced Eiko as a Japanese military scientist, that we had hired.

And then we were ready.

Eiko postulated.

"You don't suppose they tort*re space aliens out there, do you?" he asked.

"Not sure," I answered. "Why would they do anything like that?" I added, quickly.

We told them, at the military base, that we were in to see the tour. I used my American General's clout, and a very American Southerners accent.

"Name?" he asked.
"U.S. American General Thomas Lou Collins, with associates, visiting with Russian General Sonja T. Olyatov, and our guest scientist acquaintance, Eiko Eiko." I said.

And I was right. He checked. Grey Fox had added us to the list. They let us through security, and past the filing check.

"The visiting female Russian General has really good fashion sense," I heard one of them say, in his native language.
"Yeah, and she's pretty too," said one of the male office dweebs.

We were given our tour by U.S. American Lieutenant Corporal Muldave. He apparently had some German ancestry, as well, and also some light Transylvanian lineage maybe. He happily spoke in Belgian too. And later, in American English.

"First exhibit," he explained. "Space entity number one," he said. He took us through the first room. There was a large two way mirror on one side of the room, so that we could view inward.

We checked out the first space character.

It was a human female, real pretty, with reddish glares. To the side, some candles lit. And a burning pile of magazines.

Tear drops streamed down, her pretty face.

"Very good."

"Yeah," he said.

Laser vision is shut off, she said.

"Second exhibit," he pointed out. "We have another unknown space terrestrial staying in bunk number two."

I took a look, at the other space guy, that they had captured.

He had long pale slender features, with blue diamond blue eyes, and pointy ears; and some tattoos as well, with some sort of age old serpent characters, painted on his back neck and arms.

He wore the remains of a very torn leather jacket.

"Looks like another troublemaker," I said.

"Yeah, you don't want to get too close to that one," said Muldave.

"And here's our third space exhibit. The b**est maniac of the bunch." he said. "Untitled Space Wolf guy."

Sure enough, they had captured Grey Fox. They had tied him up using thick titanium cords, so that he couldn't break through the wall. Cables and electric power lines were hooked up through the wall we noticed.

"He looks very attractive," said Lady Russian General Sonja

Olyatov, in her fake Russian accent. "He seems very American to me, actually," she included. She had been referring to Grey Fox.

"Let me talk to this one, in private," I said to Muldave. I was referring to the Wolf guy.

"No," he answered.

"I'm pulling rank then," I said.

He paused for a moment. His mouth opened, slightly. He had thought it over. "Fine," he said. "I'll give you two minutes to talk to him," he said.

He opened the security doors to the third room, via an officer's key. And I entered.

"Grey Fox," I whispered to him. "It's me," I said softly.

"Herk?" Pause. "My good friend, Herk," he said.

"How did you let them do this to you?" I asked, still whispering.

"Couldn't handle them," he said. Too many shock grenades, he said. They had shock rifles too, he explained. Hurts, he said.

"Why don't you change back into human form?"

"Can't." he said, sorrowfully. "Need wolf form to survive right now. In human form, they'd shock me again," he answered. Hurts, he said again, mournfully. Hurts.

I started to cry a bit.

He had been bleeding from several cuts, and various many, at least nine, bullet wounds.

"Don't worry. We'll get you out of here," I told him.

Back at the hotel, we started to wonder.

Grey Fox was still trapped inside the military installation.
I needed to formulate a plan.

"How are we going to get him out?" asked Victorian.
"Why don't you use some of that influence of yours," I suggested.
"Maybe, I will," she said.
"Unsure," I thought. I was worried a bit.
"We could pay them off," someone else suggested.
"Not sure. They're American military. Not sure if they even take payoffs," I said.
We had represented U.S, and Russian Government, as well.
"We should also consider the tightened security angle...."
"Uh huh...." I said. "Fine," I added.

I paused a moment. Irritated, I slightly was.
"Hold up," I said. "Actually, I have a better idea," I said.

That night I packed a black satchel.

I wore a black night military outfit.

I took with me the large glock, hidden against the back of my trousers, which I covered, with my black outfit, and also a night stick, and a very fancy black switch blade number.
Also I took the satchel with me, just in case.

1948. Monday.

We drove to the military installation base, very late at night.

You two wait here, by our U.S. military truck, I instructed them. It was close to one o'clock.

I entered alone, with the satchel and my equipment.

Twenty minutes later, I came out with Grey Fox. He limped over, quite a bit.
His body still ached heavily, I could tell.
He had bullet wounds in his back too, I noticed.

Open up the f-'en truck, I whispered loudly.

They did, and I brought Grey Fox inside our military vehicle.

"How the f--- did you do that?" asked Victorian.
"I paid the night watch commander team," I said.
"How much did you pay them," asked someone else.
"Twenty million," I lied.
"But how..."
"Who knows? They'll probably make some excuse that he escaped, in the night or some sort," I suggested.
"Probably not," said Lady Victorian.
"We'll get through," I assured her. "Just drive," I said.

She gave Grey Fox a major warm hug.

And then we drove off, with Eiko behind the wheel.

About a mile down the road, we realized we had been followed. We popped the back.

I had left a surprise for them, at their car. A specialized made cannon, we used.
Their engine exploded, and they ran away screaming.

We salute you, you brave, brave U.S. American soldiers, as you did nothing, and nothing, but scream and run away, while Eiko's specialized war cannon incinerated, and pulverized, the remains of your vehicle.

We'll see you not next again hopefully, and thanks.

Thanks for the use of your time.

We love you, America!!

And that was how we got Grey Fox back home.

The night watch team had been long put to sleep.

We spent the next month and a half in Northern Main O*****, to celebrate.

And, like I said,
Thank you very much.
And, Good night.

Additional disclaimer on this chapter:

The views and opinions expressed in the above chapter do not necessarily reflect those of yours truly, Herkomar, the Great. Truly, I love Americans, and serving the United States country is totally outstandingly worthwhile.

We, all three, or four of us, made it out alive.

Thanxx!!
Yay!!!
-Herk.

36

THE 1950S

read Chronicles of Superman, female character (and lightermann) wants to be Superhero

We took a break to live Europe again for a while.

1952. Barcelona.

A new fashion trend had emerged, during the early 1950s. A new series of books had been issued. Entitled, the Chronicles of Superman, in 1938.

Lightermann had tossed me a copy of the book.

What's this? I asked him.

"Superman," he pointed out. "They're comic books," he said. "They'll make me a supra-hero," he said.

Huh? I said. These are just funny art books, I realized.

"I will, to be, a supra-hero," he announced, proudly.

Very well and good, lightermann. He had gotten into his head, that through the miracles of science, he would be able to master heroics, and fully pronounce himself into a superhuman, just like in The Chronicles of Superman, and his all-time favorite comic character, aquatic prince super-hero, Captain John W Nomar, who also fought, alongside good attractive blonde women, on the streets of New Delta City and Western Aragon.

He had even designed himself a super costume. For **Major Freedom**, as he called himself. White, blue, and *gold*, he sided, with an additional star helmet, and outfit, and with the large red lettering, MF, stickered on his chest.

"So what are you going to do now that you have a costume for yourself, lightermann?" I asked him.
"Will conduct good deeds, and fight crime," he pointed out.
"Also, for heroes," he said.

Also, he took his prize custom-designed yellow surfboard with him.

I shrugged. Lightermann was still a very good looking guy. Good-looking women thought so anyway. He still looked around twenty or twenty-two years old. He even looked slightly older and slightly more powerful, while he was wearing his superhero outfit, especially with the large surfboard.

After a while, he seemed to work out slightly more often. At certain points, lightermann could bench press over 18.9 times two hundred twenty-eight pounds.

He toured Barcelona, as a superhuman.

At later points, he went to Liverpool.

I did not doubt him, I thought.

In fact, He seemed stronger every day. And, also, we would finally be welcome back in America. -someone wants me to include.

Section ii.

Under the guise of Major Freedom, lightermann accomplished several heroic feats.

Here, I list a few.

1956.

Four good deeds that lightermann conducted as a superhero.

(1) Barcelona. He attended, and partially hosted a grand USO show, for troops from America. He toured for a series of military show offs. Performed with new tricks alongside, noted stage magician, the Great Noah, and Noah's great female assistant, Rocky Winters, who was 22. Rocky had a crush on lightermann, I bet.

(2) America. lightermann donated several rock albums to charity. He attended sports meets and concerts. He had purchased a producer credit, quickly after becoming rich and famous. He had met with famous rock producer, Chet Armstrong, to discuss enhancing image, and images, which lightermann was more than proud to integrate into his projects. Afterwards he took Donna Jay Herkomar to a ballgame, in which he dressed in a light casual version of his costume. Happily, he waved, and ate heartily of the various sports concessions. He held up his surfboard proudly.

(3) England. He also tested a jet pack that he himself, had constructed, and also a rocket launcher, developed by our scientist. They ran a series of tests. He'd rocket through, slowly, and lightly set himself down.

The jet pack quickly became his favorite. He'd brag about this all the time.

(4) England. Endorsement of dark and yellow chip bar. Lightermann was approached by a corporate to run a series of commercials, featuring a corporate brand chip bar. A series of commercials ran. He opened the yellow and dark chip wrapper. O'Hannigan's Chip Bar., it read. Through this offer he was able to make money, additionally. He wore his vinyl spandex costume when he could.

What are your powers, lightermann? Lady Victorian once asked him. She had recently secured a line conducting tasks for the Grand Apple Force.

"The power to be good," was lightermann's answer.

As a prank, a female someone purchased a bunny rabbit outfit for him later.

For a while, he went on the open road, with his costume and his gold surfboard, and his bunny outfit.

"I am good, very super, very surf board hero, right now." he said.

For him, that made his endearing venture all well worth it.

Also,
I'll add more to this chapter later, maybe. If I want to.

Section iii.

1958.
Close to Nazi Central America.

Ousterforth paused. He took a break, to open up his canteen. He guzzled the water, and then went for a snack pack. He had been working his way through the long warm Central American jungle.

He had been cutting through vines. Long and hard. He sweated. He took his hat off for a moment. Wiped the sweat off his brow.

The party had lost him for over two days.
However, thankfully, he recovered. They'd never know he was gone, with the gold packs.
The snakebite did not hurt him.

After all that, he'd become wealthy.

Section iv.

So what else is Herkomar up to?

1958. California. We had eventually been let back in America.

I got a new hot job working at a new model agency.

There had been a steady supply.

Here's a memo I wrote.

1959.

The days are long and pleasantly enjoyable. I'm working valiantly on several lucrative business projects to mind the time. For that, work will receive better, and time will be better reserved. For those days I contemplate joining an additional artists field. With Love. All that had been marvelously made for design and well thought out commission.

I saw an ad across the street for women's dark leggings. Startling was the level of bright color boldness. The matter seemed well and pleasant. I also felt a certain degree of stateliness from watching the cars drive by, on the interstate, quickly. Yes, I agreed. They moved quite quickly and with a good system of excellence and thoughtful arrival

Time seems to be moving faster, I realized.

Thanks!!
Herkomar.

I did a large packet afterwards. And I had fallen in love with the good world all over again.

We set well and took good placement as an advertising studio. I

took to designing wall brochures. We marketed the color print cata-
logs well, and distributed using our good factory made label. They
had manufactured and produced for color quick print, and tech-
nique. The lighting fixtures were cool, and kept us well in business.
We generally kept cool. Our conditioning kept us cool, wet, and dry.
With good theory and good excellence, perhaps our futures were all
the brighter for it. The mass production of our technologies, felt a
safer mode of human invention and bright initiation.

The world had kept us stronger and in better condition.
The cars glide forth, with uniform system and fulfillment.

1961. I later realized.

Some say, around the 1980s, they started adding neon lighting.

End chapter.

37

THE 1960S, AND THE 1970S

build rocket; Victorian and Grey Fox become involved with peace movement

1968. For a while, we focused on the new project.

The Soviet government had recently been sending astronauts into space. I had consulted Eiko about this.

"Can we do something like this?"
He thought this over a bit.
"Give it at least a month and a half," he said.

That's fine, I figured.
We ordered more tech parts from the catalog.

Ten months later. The plans had been finished.

The rocket, actually, was modeled after most others.

"Are these the missiles, we have scheduled?" I asked him.
"It's a rocket," he explained. He flipped the safety cover over.
Then he pressed the button on his hand remote.
The rocket launched.
A new monitor watched the daily.

Towards the sky, the rocket blasted upwards with tremendous force.

"Can we make it go from side to side," I asked.
"Yeah, but why?" he said.
"Oh...I gotcha," I realized.

We checked the counter. Apparently, our rocket ascended at least twelve miles upward.
"It's good," pointed out Malory. He tapped the stationing equipment lightly.

When complete, an ejection auto, went off. And the parts of the rocket, floated to the ground. We went to check on the remnants. By car, we drove four miles to the landing site.

The small calico kitten who we selected, to man the operation (from inside the rocket), had totally survived.

"Maow...," it said. It licked me on the cheek.

"Next, maybe we can send lightermann to space too," I suggested.
"Maybe," said Eiko, and he put the remains of the rocket away, in truck. I placed the kitten back in her set, where she mewled happily. Purr, she said.

1968. Austin.

I had another talk with my daughter, Donna J. Herkomar, after that.

She was the official sixth member of Team Five, we had decided at some point.

Quite often, she, our career girl, would return from a hard day of work.

Donna, you just have to focus harder, I told her.

You have no idea, Herkomar, she said to me. My friends called me 'Herkomar'.

At a certain point during the mid-1900s, Donna had become highly involved with a new club. She had originally been identified, and recruited by them, in the year 1908. Apparently, they had been a group nomm'ed the Jay Murtaugh-McHennessey Finance Group, and they had been very highly interested in my daughter.

Originally, she explained to me, they had set up distribution farms and factories in Russia, which spread out later to France, and Italy, and New Zealand, and various countries and continents. They purported to enforce clean business services.

Interesting, her story was. I did a look up.

The facts all seemed to check out. Apparently, they seemed fairly decent.

She attended numerous meetings of theirs, and from that, they managed to leak her sizeable funds, in exchange for extended work services for them.

1972.

She came from another rough day at the office.
Hon, it's important. You have to work hard, I explained to her.

You and Eiko don't work hard, she said, or stated.
Slight pause.
"We have money," I explained to her.

She took a break, and left the room, probably to fix herself a cheese sandwich and some milk.

Some days I worried about her. Although, she had been very nice and pleasant, recently, I guess.

1973.

After two years, Donna experienced a good deal of personal and financial success. She made her fortunes in several decent ways, she mentioned to me.

The kitten had survived too, as well, I guess.

1976.

Meanwhile, Grey Fox and Lady Victorian had become involved with the peace movement, somewhere focused in London.

I asked her about this later.

Apparently, they held several anti-war demonstrations, she explained to me.
Also, together they attended certain peace-making treaty operations.

And afterwards, then, they would have embrace in better fashion.

She even appeared on the modern style telle-visor for a while.

"We just want all the violence to stop," she announced, on broadcast, calmly, and rationally.

Lady Victorian embraced Grey Fox and his magnificent body. She held him there, for hours, and for long and longer, until she was totally reassured by his peace market, for that day.

You have no idea how wonderful you are sometimes, she said to him. She gave him a long kiss, afterwards. And he stood there, holding her.

1979. Is there anyone else I'm forgetting?

Oh, yeah, that's right. Lightermann, of course.

Under the guise of Major Freedom, lightermann continued to fight crime in the street of Burbank, California, until 1988.
Among the populous, he had become a known enforcement tool.
He had recently stopped a robbery at a pawn shop, by combat jabbing a gun runner hard across the shoulder, and kicking him a few times so that it hurt way bad.

Someone made a phone call about this incident.

A reporting service came in to interview him.

"What's next in store for Major Freedom?" A cute pretty dark-haired reporter asked him, during interview.

"Will continue to make London great. For truth, justice, and the American way," came Major Freedom's response.

Good comeback, I thought.

He sure did make us proud, we all knew.

He bit into an O'Hannigan's chewy chip bar. Yum, he said.

Very praiseworthy job, lightermann, we figured.

"Freedom's just another word, for, Nothing left to lose, And it's Nothing, and it's Nothing, if it ain't free...." -1978.

And the long story, of Team Five continues.

End of chapter.

38

THE 1980S, AND THE 1990S

funeral for a friend co-worker friend; and then, the 1990s; parody of a Christmas carol

The 1980s.

1982.

A friend of ours passed away. He, Neilmeyer, expired along with his wife.

We all showed for the funeral.

Joe Brantly stood solemnly, attired in his total dark formal attire.

Even Lightermann attended, as requested. He had worked with Neilmeyer extensively, as well.

Neilmeyer had been one of our closest dearest comrades.

He had done ops for our east coast manufacturers-side.

One day, they had gone off for a trip, cross country.
Their car had been hit by an autobus.

How much was it worth, someone asked, at a recreation bar, later.
I did not know how to answer. I drank from a club soda.

The sports screen skipped a bit. We tightly monitored for passing new land information.

For a while we took a break....

1984. Early Christmas, sixteen days before.

I went out for a cold drink, highly caffeinated, and a poetry club.
My daughter also did poetry, as well.

Josselyn, to the left, off stage:

As far as I know, this is the earliest I've been here,
From what I can tell there will always be more...

And I cherish you all in great advance.
The Song of Three Ghosts.

clap, clap, clap, clap....,

I drank from the bottle.

1985.

I woke up at 5:15 in the morning.
Lightermann needed to be driven to the airport again, for his visit to San Anna.

I called him a cab, and then crawled back to sleep.

1985. Ten minutes later.

Lightermann: "I can't find my adaptor cord," he said.
What the f***, I thought.

"Buy a new one," I suggested.

1987. Years after.

And we still wake up in America, for a while.

For the morning, I fix a shot of cola, for myself, with some ice in it.

1988. Eleven days before Christmas.

I ditched the board room meeting early.

"Where's he going?" asked a female corporate.
"Who knows."
Pause.
"Leave him alone. It's his own business anyway," someone else commented.

I packed up my duffel bag, and prepared to leave the office for the Friday afternoon.
Lady Vi was out, visiting Singapore, on vacation, that day.

There was a brief pause, to focus in the hallway of our offices.
I searched, out the long window. I touched the glass, closely.

First Ghost: Constiglione.

He, Constiglione: "It's not the end of the world, you know...."
I turned, very slightly.

But Constiglione was no longer there, I had expected.

He had left us, over a century ago.

And then there he was.

And then, there he was.

He stood to the left, of myself.

Constiglione, our dearest friend: "Herkomar," he said. "Tonight we will revisit the past."

"But why," I asked him.

"To illustrate," was the answer. -Constig.

We went through at least a dozen peace sessions.

1673.

Constiglione: played late night on the viola gamba strings.

"How long will this take," asked Fiona.

"A dozen days or so."

"Should we ask him before hand?"

"No, please, but I care about him. He is my good friend," remarked Constiglione. He continued his work.

1537.

I cried. In the snow I cried.

Me: I was very lonely back then.
Constiglione: Yes. Of course. It is early on.
Me: Sorry, I always regretted.
"Thank you," he said.

1781.

Lightermann is studying. He is studying hard.

Later he gives good thanks to the world.

1793.

Those were, of course, for us, The Age of Reason.

The years went by, for which, we focused onwards.

1468.

Lady Victorian is sleeping in bed. She thinks of Herkomar. Quite often.

Her figure is warm and comforting. Her bedding is exquisite and prominently made.

1488.
We took a break in the parlor.

1641.
I had another snack pack.

Constiglione took another drink, a blue-red drink.

I remember -he remembers- the early world very fondly.

1643. England.

Me: Are there more out there?
Constiglione: Yes. I say, yes.

Very well, I thought.
"Enjoy," he promised.

1819. And so, we look into the bold.

1873. We look into the bold.

1988.

And there was another gift, from him, for that day.

Second ghost: Napoleon.

Me: Are you of course the sage?
I am, of course, Napoleon, he said.

I nodded. We were civil.

1995.

Here we are. Here we are in the 1990s.

1995. We sent up another rocket.

We figured, for that, for the matter that was worth it.

1996. Donna is griping. Lightermann has made another television appearance.

"Donna, I don't have time," I said to her.

Sorry, I said.

2006.

And there will always be some good granted.
Said Herkomar, she said.

1877.

"Do you want to go for another ship," Happy Jack Davenport asked me.
"No, not right now," I said, cool.
He nodded, sort of.
"They say it's better, if you buy early," he said.
"I said, not right now." And I gave him a very cold look.

You were slightly rude to Happy Jack, I thought, he said.

Me: Yeah, maybe. Yeah.

I nodded.
Me: Maybe I should have treated Happy Jack nicer.
Constiglione: Uh huh.

In The Oceanika Hotel, Sao Paul*?, MA; or Monte Carlo. Bridge.

Total Celebrations.

We had worked out the extra finance costs.

A female share leader agreed.

Did you ever miss Alice, by the way? he asked.

Yeah, I thought. Sometimes, I mentioned.

1988. Present day. The Americas.

I continued my focus, at the streets outside the window pane.
A fast car beeped.

I spent the rest of the day with Alexia.
Later.

2008. Me and Alexia. Marivale, Ohio.

We kissed. I held her in my arms, that evening.

The Americas.

We powdered our drinks, afterwards.

2037. We all took another break.

There had been a new concert in town, which I attended.

The Arrow Space, Incorporates.

Yeah, Can you dig it, someone asked.

Yeah, I thought so. I sure could.

1993-1994. Eiko was still designing new future technologies. He had renewed a new operations contract. Then we were testing the new super computer which he had purchased.

"These computers are built to last," he explained.
Very good, I thought.

We named our new super computer JETHRO 1900.

We tested the handling extensively.
The prompt keys worked well enough. Eager to please, the computer seemed, and very user friendly.

1998. After that, we sent up another rocket.

We figured, for that, for the matter that was worth it.

2016. Present day. Future. Dinner at La Waldens.
We looked over.

I ordered the Dip Sandwich, aus jus.
She ordered the teriyaki steak.

We made pleasant conversation.

"I guess now that we're completed," I said to her.
"I know, Herkomar," she said. She bit into a thin strip of steak.
"Sorry if I'm not the same, as I used to be, sometimes." she said.
"I know how you feel," I brought this up.
"Pleasant after dinner, right?"
"I suppose."
"Oh, you are so awesome, Herkomar." she said.
"I love that bit you do, by the way," I mentioned.

"*Thank* you. Thank you so much, *sweetie.*" She said.

2039. Alexia and I sat together in the lounge space.

We should go to the rooftop some time.
It's so much better when Donna's not causing an issue, she said.
I smiled and concurred.

At a certain point, I really should have married Alexia.

Me: Can they see us? I asked.
Nap.: Maybe. There are, of course many good-looking women.

Me: I love you, Napoleon. I said to him.

1994. Present day. Modern.

We picked up again. We picked up quite nicely.

The new contracts had succeeded, and we had all moved forth.

Do you want to see more, they asked me.
Sure, I said, most certainly.

Third ghost: Christensen.

We waited patiently, and he arrived.

2151-2180.
We look into the bold.

Donna: "But, daddy....we need more *money*...."

2041.

"We are here, of course to show you the new."

I started to cry, for slightly a moment.

Sobbing, I guess.

2043. Present day. Modern.

Donna is asking me for a new data-porter.

Node....

2048.

"We'll get one later," added Christensen.

2118.

And.
It's said:
Our captain, our captain, is no longer there.

What's to become?, said darling....

2187. Present day. Modern.

Alexia starts crying. Her main suit friend, Herkomar, is gone....

In Fairmont, west, II. On the High Heavenly, Beachside.

"The grand audience is waiting," she said.

"Very well."

The new butler, Neil, then brought forth her new arrangement items.

2018. April.
In Hannebar. Trondheim.

"It's a matter of wise investment," explained Constiglione.
A very pretty young woman smiled.

"You look so cute, Constiglione," Elle. Lyndia said.

2146. Modern.

At the main gallery:

"...and handsome in the future."

Christensen nodded. He fiddled with a good coin.

A gold-level attendee nodded in agreement.

This had been a major event. Apparently we made deal over a thrilling new feature.

2282.

Eiko is manufacturing a new tech device.

That's what I heard.
Wholesome is the capacity.

1831. Still. Lelend is working steady.
"Yes," said someone.

And I agreed.

1927.

Christensen stands, powerful and tall.
His loyal cadre stays silent. There appears to be six or seven, or eight of them.

Gren****** places his hand. He holds his hand atop the gaffing box.

It's 1936, or so.

And...
Also.

1988.

A fast car beeped.

2061.

Ashford. De-Sirca. Lenny, a new colored friend of ours, smiled. He drank from a bottle of He-rum champagne.

2073.

We held the celebration in February.

2123.

There was more to that legend, she said.

I praised Sara, I thought.

The whole world seemed for a point, marvelous. We took another dip of cola. Sweet and pure, it felt on the tip of my tongue.

How I loved and enjoyed and praised majesty, in total.

2156.

"Just what would your father say, Donna," she asks her.
"But I don't care," she coldly remarks.

Donna grabs her jacket and her set of golf clubs, and then she leaves.

And more.

2071.

"Why the h' did we get beta colony...?"
"Shut the f--- up," said Mitch.

Grenwalder nods. He orders a complete packet.
And then the time option says more, says Stephanie Waynebrau.

And I concur, fully, says Christensen.

This is 2137, they say.

2148.

We still go forward.

2236.

Our new stocks had rose. We were gaining more.

We gladly accepted at the main file conference.

2241.

We saw the Great Building, and Epic in Monument. Towering, it was.
For a while I stood there, as if I had conquered.

The water ran into the pool. The blue, the gorgeous blue...

A young blonde-haired woman, in a very modern fashionable outfit, stands.
Her mind anticipates.

2278.

Pleasant, said the afternoon.

2390. Mars. Colony Three.

I gladly accepted the new peace ring.

"The new peace ring," she asked.
"It's sort of a ring token."
"It's a pledged acceptance of the new globe environments," I said.

2391.

The Grace Estate Tower looked awesome in the moonlight.

Astonishing. Simply breathtaking.

We stared upon, the garden lawn, astonished.
And captivated.

The Golden Idol says:
"And more to the future."

"And more to the future...."

And more to the future....

And more.

Jupiter....

The Great Many Moons of New Saturn.

Orbit. Eighty-four, Twenty-four, thirty-seven....
Orbit...

Orbit....

And more....

And more....

And more.

Long pause....

2489.

And this is where we stopped for a moment....

2489.

And this is where we stopped.

2489.

To Alpha Nobilis....

2489.

Star Cluster seventeen. To Great Grand New Luxury.

2489.

A beat....

And also...

A beat....

And also...

A beat....

And a beat.... And a beat. And so.

And again....

2489. The Hill sector Fronts. New Satyrn. Upper west. Stationed.

And, well, also, # 4:
Another very good-looking attractive middle-aged blonde woman is having dinner with her family.

The well-dressed maid, I Victorian serves a plate of roast duck, with gold honey sauce.

I still miss Herkomar, she thinks.

The attractive blonde woman eyes her, suspiciously.

"What are we going to do about the new prime Arielle survey?" asks a young woman. She seems around twenty-four years of age. Who, is this younger woman? They ask. Donna, I think, properly.

The attractive older blonde woman stays silent for a moment. While that, she wipes her mouth carefully. She waits for some more. She helps herself to a good drink of rose-colored wine.

And then,
"We'll pick up after the next shipment," she finally agrees.

The younger woman, her, nods.
The family is quite pleased.

They cheer, very softly.

Happy Christmas, they say.

1988. And then the spirits are gone.

And also, the third future spirit had left as well.

1988. We follow through.

1988.

I stared out the glass for a moment.

And then I grabbed my duffel bag and headed off the office level.

1988.

I hailed a taxi in the street.

"Watch it," said a street runner.

I paused, slightly.

1994. The Present Industrial.

"How was the meeting," asked Alexia. She was always concerned.

The meeting was pertinent, I thought.

I gave her a hug.

Alexia felt so warm in my arms.

1996. A quiet evening alone, with Alexia.

I took her to a restaurant.

Together, we commence.

1996. September.

In the next evening, I awoke.

1998. More then, I picked up some goods from the pick-up station.

Handily, I wore my sunglasses.

What's that new music playing on the band station, I asked.
"Probably a new band," someone said.
I thought it over for a bit, and then agreed. Times were changing, music was very slightly improving, for this time. Gladly, we would forge the future.

Casually, I bought a box of extra glazed donuts, and chip sandwiches: For the crew, at (our) home base, back in Austin.

Maybe, I thought.

We'll see how it turns out in the next four decades, someone reminded me.

They were still moving new technology towards the hub. The motors went faster. Our new devices soared. They carried our name brand, quite well.

1998. Mid-Late December. And so, we all had our mission base Christmas dinner party. For NASS'ER (National Aeronautics Space Organization and Operations).

At love central, we enjoyed.
And everyone was invited. And lightermann.
I held my darling, Alexia, close.

Even A'Jax Constiglione was placed on the invitation list, for that year. This champagne is really good, someone said. It's non-alcoholic, I pointed out.

End of chapter.

PART VI

Future Modern IV

Future Modern IV

2020s-story about the future

2030s-they decide to film a movie

2040s-(Note: At this point scientists have found a cure for death.)

39

THE 2020S

story about the future

So there we were, in the year 2021.

The Americas.

Together, we well established.

We sat in the diner, and had a good meal.

I ordered the steak burger, of course.

Donna ordered a cold soft drink.

Welcome to the new millennium, we thought.

"So how's your mother," I asked her.
"She's handling well. She made another success," reported Donna.

"Another success, that's very good."
"They're thinking of promoting her."
"Well, that's good for all of us, I guess," was my answer.
"I know," she said.

I chewed a fry chip. She slurped her beverage.

I waited at the car stop.

They picked me up in the Rolls around 11:23, that night.

"We just wanted to report to you, good job," said Ecclestone.
"It's a big star with the media reports," reported Nick.
"That sounds great," I said. I moped a bit. I sat in the back of the limo.
"What are you worried about, Herkomar? You should be pleased. Your product deal is Grade O-good ," asked Nick.
"Leave him be for a moment," said Ecclestone. "He's processing real quick right now, maybe," Ecclestone added.

They drove me to my four star mansion house.

"We'll see you on Monday, Herkomar," called Ecclestone.
"See you later."

I took the rest of my burgers with me.

I picked up a caffeinated beverage from the home drink server. "Drink served," said the server, in a low baritone voice.

"Thank you, Robot," I said.

Blonde fitness model: D'Anica Jordan lounged by the pool. She had waited up.

"So how was lunch?" she asked.
"Pleasant." I said.

All I need is you, I said to her.

After a while, we lightly danced the night away.

Perfect.

9:14. Saturday.

The next morning, I awoke. Things seemed lightly different. I checked the oxygen level, by the pool.
This seems vaguely ordinary, I thought.

I checked D'Anica. She was still asleep, in bed.

On the television, the news. Apparently, a meteorite had struck, somewhere local. Also, there was an article, of a strong diver's convention, in town.

I skipped through the channels, lightly.

I called up my friend, Max.

"Max, did you feel a slight air spike last night." Apparently, a meteorite fell last night.

That's right. He explained. The meteorite strike initiated a transshift, a science change. It's similar to cosmic cycles, he said. The air is a little different today. I thought about this. Noted, and I agreed.

Thank you, I said. That was my conversation with him.

I took the rest of the day off, I figured. D'Anica took off, as well. She had to handle some light work issue at her catalog office; or conduct a drop-by, or similar.

For part of the afternoon, I watched quick classic 1900s science fiction, on the air. This work had been influenced by our own government-sanctioned network stations, for part, they suggested. Playing: A science fiction show about a guy and his female cyborg sidekick.

The duo attend meeting with their boss, the chief, who is also a blonde female model type, and wearing a cool corporate style dress outfit. During the meeting, the cyborg sidekick gets up to pick up a long sandwich from a cart.

"This show is awesome," she says, while sitting in a futuristic bean bag-style chair.

"Thank you, cyborg sidekick," says the blonde female commissioner.

I went through some of my old records. Popular hits by the Silver Cruz Band. They had released at least three albums, in my collection. And their classic hit single: Love Streaker.

I myself was a big fan of the first album (and also their second album, By the River). Their third album was well received, critically and somewhat mildly acclaimed. However, I didn't have time to listen, to all three albums, at that point.

I played their second album, twice in a row.

Afterwards, I did a light workout, and went for a swim in the pool.

I walked around the luxury mansion, wearing a towel, for a half hour or so.

My muscles felt very strong.

That night we out for a dinner, at O'Shea's. We took a crowd of three or four, including D'Anica, and two other very good-looking women.

I ordered a large micro-pizza, with some burger topping.

The women ordered what they wanted.
Satisfied, we were with life.

Then we headed went back to my omega light modern mansion, where we wholesomely partied quite a bit.

Time flew.
D'Anica, and her friends headed off, after hours.

The air felt clearer. Some of us felt stronger.

I took another dip in the pool.

And that was the day, the meteorite struck our area.

2026. We lived stronger. And we lived, for more.

End chapter.

Also....
Bonus: Brief Interlude III-

Additional scene with Grey Fox. Seattle 2027.

Grey Fox: Herkomar, did you take my box of double mint cookies?

Herkomar: Why, no, of course, I didn't take your box of double mint cookies. (pause) I'm not even sure, about what they look like.

Grey Fox: Are you sure? They're sort of round-shaped chocolate chip cookies, and they're filled with fresh double mint.

Herkomar: Well, gee, um, I, um, I sort of don't know.

Grey Fox: Uh huh. Yep. They look a lot like that box of double mint cookies, that I saw you and chassady, eating last week.

Herkomar: Well, um, fine, I guess, I guess I'll be sure to keep my eyes open for them.

Grey Fox: Uh huh. *(pause.)* I was keeping them in the pantry.

Grey Fox sits down on the couch. He opens a beer bottle, blue ribbon quality. Then he switches the channel onto sports. Football plays on the big screen.

Herkomar: Well, I'll let you know, if I find them.

Grey Fox (he says): Thanks, Herkomar. You're the greatest.

Grey Fox watches the good-looks team cheerleaders showcase their movements on television. He takes a few glugs.

Herkomar hides the box of fresh double mint cookies that he has stashed under his new burgundy member's jacket.

Scene ii.

Herkomar: We may need to invest more, on the high upper grand's end.

Triumphe: Is that what they've been saying, man?

And, the conclusion...

End of Interlude.

40

THE 2030S

they decide to film a movie

2034-2038. United States, Italy. Iceland.
And, The Netherlands.

At a certain point, we decided to stretch our productive energies, on a new project.

Lady Vi. had found the screenplay. Entitled, The Great Nobler World: The Greater Adventures of Joan of Arc.
I glanced it over, a bit.

"I'll only produce your movie," I said to her, "...if I can put my girlfriend, Alexia, in one of the lead parts," I said.

This met her approval.
I contacted Alexia, she was most interested.

We granted her for the role of a blonde female angel, Ariel, complete with white wings. She communicates with Joan, approximately one third of the way through the film's length.

Our sound coordinator was Eiko.

We hired lightermann to work in the props department.

For the role of Joan, herself, there was a dispute. Tim, our screen captain, had a very pretty female model friend, with very dark hair, and simply extraordinary and exquisitely enticing blue eyes. Diana, her name was. She was only fourteen years old yet she looked simply breathtaking for that age. Clearly, a model, we knew.

We took a bunch of screenshots of her, in various elegant blue wardrobe. The crew liked her quite a bit.

Afterwards, I consulted with a friend of mine, who worked for the clergy.

He suggested we use the alternate choice, who I myself then selected as a fore-runner for the role of Joan of Arc.
We cast a total red haired actress, Kathleen White, for the role of Joan herself.

She whispered something smart in my ear, during the filming.

I selected Kathleen over. She probably looked more relatable to Christian audiences, my clergy man friend said.

We kept the screenshots of Diana, anyway. And we used her for another bit in our movie, to play Joan's younger cousin, incidentally named Diana, also, as well.

Anyway....

Open Credits. The Greater Adventures of Joan of Arc.

Scene four.

> Joan
> It started in Maspeth in 1422.
> The battles raged on. Crops were burned.
> Women were alerted.
> Soldiers were buried.
>> (beat)
> The time came for a new order.
>> (beat)
> My name is Joan of Arc.
>> (beat)
> And Truly I would lead the Great Revolution.

Opening shot: a battlefield. Wounded men thrown aside.

The beautiful Joan of Arc stands peacefully in metal armor.

She looks outward wearing her battle gear, and her leather outfit.

She motions to the side.

The scene (continues).

Scene two:
I ate a large cruller pastry right in front of the camera crew.

"Does this bother you guys," I asked.

"That's groovy," one of the extras said to me.
Then I downed a cold cup of coffee, with a lot of sugar in it.

I gave Alexia a kiss. She looked gorgeous, as always.

"Do you want to be in our movie, Herkomar?" Victorian asked
me.
"Nah, it's fine," I said. I had thought it over a bit.

"I'd actually like to be in the movie," she herself said.
"Fine," I said. We cast her as Countess Bree, one of the count-
esses that we had hired, for the production.
Great, I decided.

We went out for more coffee.

Then we had a few intimacy rounds later. Nicely, we connected.

We tested the recording equipment.

I had Lady Victorian read lines.

Also, we taped her, sipping on a cup of cold soda.

Production continued.

Q: How long was the shoot?

A: At least three months. We took careful time and preparation to get the movement of the scenes right. It was a pretty good movie, once we completed it. It initially screened in at least two hundred theaters. For our production company, cleverly named: Immortal Productions. We considered our piece a brilliantly timed epic. I myself re-wrote the script, at least twice, I'll add.

We received some major results from our film.

Scene Fifteen:

Interior. Horse Stable.

Guy, the stable boy, is working.

He realizes that Joan has entered.

Guy StoneBreaker
So, how's it going, Joan? What's in, for the next day?

Joan
Nicely. Quite nicely. Pleased that you have a very good insight on the world....

They talk, peacefully.

Scene continues. Endlessly, it seems.

After a while the film progressions became an exciting new challenge.

I'd wake up in the morning feeling great. I'd down a lace of cola, and be off to work early. The whole crew was brilliant. Our effects team had film effects totally mastered. We even hired a few work interns from Paris Tech.

They brought in a whole bunch of extra, and in the day shoots, we'd watch the actresses rehearse their lines.

Scene Twenty-Six.

Ext. The battlefield.

Joan fights with all her might.

Joan
We fight the world as heroes. Together we stand.

Epically, chosen. Herself, she stands proudly. Brandishing her sword.

Ariel
Ho what greater champions announced.

Jack Hale
Here, here.

And the battle resumes.

Joan swings proudly. Her sword cuts open, opposing soldiers.

As we cleared through the skirmishes, we found our glorious work come together.

Scene Sixty Four

Int. Colombian Palace.

Joan dines with dinner celebrities.

Shaker Red
And to what good nature, did you find?

Joan

We apparently, encountered greater high life.

Shaker Red

Pleasantly splendid.

Joan

Yes. Indeed. Thank you. My liege.

They continue to dine.
Joan takes a bite of white meal.

Scene continues.

With that, we cheered on.

Great noble, she was.

I must say, at a certain point, the director really knew what she was doing. I have to hand it to Lady Vi. She really knew high quality. She had been fairly well laced, around the studio set.

Even lightermann played a role. He placed the character, Ravermore, a visiting dignitary sent to present gifts, alongside Kathleen.

When we cast him, I suppose we sort of knew what we were do-ing. He was approached by a modeling agency, afterwards.

Lightermann really was a good-looking guy. All the good-look-ing women thought so.

Scene One Hundred Four.

Int. Loft Castle

Joan presents gifts. Included is an array of gold, and a sterling silver saber (long diamond sword).

> Countess Helen
> To what good service is all this?

> Joan
> To your astute greatness, and royalty. We will fight honorably by your side, Countess.

Ravermore nods. He gives a good thumbs up.

In the background: A woman angel smiles.

And more continued.

Gladly, we displayed the high quality of our studio.
-Herkomar

The film ends with Joan, very lightly wounded, and resting, on the battlefield. She apparently wins, and survives, the battle of Rouen.

Her final lines:

Joan
Please keep this world for me, my lovely.

She is carried off by one of her stronger handsome young male suitors. He raises his arm, and places a large battle sword on the battlefield.

The audience cries.

A red and blue and white banner waves.

And then?
Roll end credits.

I have to mention how involved in filming, we were, at points.

When I thought of the original Trinity, it was only me and Lady Vi, for a while.

Typically, some days.

Signed,
Herkomar

Additional notes:

The final cut of our Joan of Arc series was edited and released in 2034. It ran at least 126 minutes.

Together, we made at least 148 million dollars off our independent production venture.

Listed by Weld Ford Magazine June or April 2039.

End chapter.

41

THE 2040S

**Note: At this point scientists
have found a cure for death.**

Note: Oh, and by the way, this is basically the end of our book. I just wanted to say, I thank you. I thank you, dear readers, and I hope the world is useful.

The reason why this book stops here, is at this point, in the 2040s, immortality is nothing rare, and scientists have found a cure for death, as mentioned, in the title of this chapter.

Team Five was useful, for purposes of identifying artifact works.

However, by 2019, scientists developed a miracle drug, called, "steeg", quite often, a highly advanced steroid that could prevent aging in all good and decent human subjects. We still used cola, of course, but we used these drugs, *steeg*, also, as well. The substance was made generally available in solid form.

2028. Early on, they had marketed this as an over the counter drug initially. Then later, after very successful testing and superior results, in which 'steeg' had proven safe and effective, they, the manufacturers, even put this new immortality drug in caffeinated consumer soft drink beverages, and all various drink and cigarette products; so that we all could live longer, live stronger, and heal faster. Normal, it seemed most all of could live to at least over a hundred and forty years of age. And even longer, very many, many scientists predicted.

After a while, there were noticeable effects.

Women consumers in their sixties and eighties, looked to be in their twenties and thirties.

We looked buffer, stronger, and more sculpted, more beefed up, on muscle steroids, hormone enhancing substance agents, and more intelligent, hooked up, totally, on brain steroids, and 'steeg'.

Steroids, and super caffeine and enhancers, had become the key. At once, they had saved, and restored, the planet basically.

No longer were we alone, as immortals. By 2036, one out of every eleven individuals, tested to be a true immortal with the capacity to live longer than eighty seven or eighty eight years of age.

Amazing, truly, was the general reaction. We lived longer, and worked faster.

We now had a larger pool of applicants.

Money was to be made, and we all made it.

Technology had been perfected.

Early food and cocaine synthesizer technologies, were marketed around the 2010s, by the way. By 2035, we had access to all the newer greater science machines, including super nanode technology, and high Q-VR holodrive technology.

───◆───

In 2041.

By 2046, we rocked.

Every day, we grew, and evolved further. And remembered more.

Scientists estimated, that in ten more years, we'd reach another high quality apex.

───◆───

And, so that's then where we end. In 2048. In modern Oceania.

Thousands, or millions, of humans, around the globe, had become qualified immortals, as well.

───◆───

"Do you need help with that sandwich?" someone asked. It had been made of barbeque pork.

───◆───

Many Tributes:

Thanks to Grey Fox.

Thanks to Lady I. Victorian

And lightermann, of course.

And Thanks to Eiko, as well.

Also, I'd like to give a very important thanks to Hanna and Constiglione. For helping me complete my important book journal, with their important trust.

And, to my daughter, Donna, who still looks eighteen, and who I appreciate more and more these days.

2048. In New Portland. Australia.

We all headed for the restaurant, the five or six of us, and chewed our dinners, in well spirits.

Remainder of the Team Five.

"What's on the new horizons," someone asked.
"Somehow, we all manage, and we all live longer," I guess, and I figured deeply, as well.

I ordered another cola, my second or third. I'll let lightermann do the wrap up, maybe, I suppose.

Thank you.

Anyhow.

Thank you, dear reader,
And, Very Much Obliged.

Your beloved Narrator,
-Herkomar

End of chapter.

EPILOGUE
FUTURE MODERN
IV-(THE 2080S???)

notes and annotations by lightermann; additional; by Herkomar lightermann tells the story of the shark

First off, I, lightermann, would like to clear up a few misconceptions, and also tell a few stories. Herkomar has requested, I write a strong afterward for his journal book. Here, I have completed my annotations.

Written by lightermann.

Act I-Coming of Age

In the early and mid to late 1500s, these days were not so bad for me. Herkomar reported I was caught wandering the streets. However, he didn't mention that I did have a place to stay overnight. There was a day stack warehouse, where the general manager felt he could trust me, so he let me stay in the warehouse, over night. So I did have a place to sleep. "Very good, lightermann. I approve. Good job."-Herk.

Also, there was a good-looking young woman in Sweden. She was from a high aristocratic family; and she sort of thought I was nice-looking, and she thought I was very pleasing. She'd bring me some light beige snacks, sometimes. Beige snacks? Wha? They're like bread snacks, explains lightermann.

She'd bring me some light beige snacks, sometimes and food provisions, and water, and also she'd sneak me, some money too, very good. Her name was Kajsa. "Here are some more light beige snacks, vandergaard," she'd say to me. She was very, very pretty. Later, her family moved, and she had to move too. I miss Kajsa sometimes. "Oh, this is sort of a sad for me, lightermann. It's still very cute though. There was a pretty girl, even back when, who had a crush on you too."-says Herkomar.

Act II-Gathering Soldiers and Allies

Also, as far as thing were concerned, once discovered by Herkomar's group, I only met Hanna, like five or six times. I didn't know her that well. I heard recently, that she was selected to be captain of a space shuttle, later in the 1900s.

"Uh, I'm not sure where you heard this information. Who's to know? I was under the impression that Hanna simply left our societies. I didn't hear this same rumor you heard, so I won't, and shouldn't, debate you on this one bonus aditional-offered factoid."-Herk

On the 1600s and the 1700s. I don't know why, I mention, I actually could speak more than two or three languages, like Herkomar writes. At college I later learned at least six additional languages, and how to translate them. "This information is probably true, now I realize. Maybe I could've noted this better."- says Herk. "He knew the languages, quite well, in fact." He says.

Act III-The Story About the Shark (II)

Herkomar tells the truth sometimes. But there's a story he left out. One day, in the 1780s, I was standing on the prow of a boat, off the coast of the East Mediterranean. Accidentally, I slipped in the waters. While underwater, a shark attacked me. I took out my scabbard, and I slew into the shark, in the shark's eye. I had killed the shark. I felt very bad about this. I grabbed the rope, and they pulled me up. Later, I cried. I cried because, I had killed something.

I confessed to her later.

Lady Victorian held me in her arms for two hours after that. "Oh, lightermann. Will you ever learn."-thanks.

Act IV-Days of Battle Glory/ And The Moments of Truth (III)

The 1800s were always a good decade. We had certain fiestas, and I went out on the Wild Western.

In the 1900s, I also accomplished other feats as a superhero, in action, that Herkomar did not list.
-lightermann
For instance, one day, under the guise of Major Freedom, my personal assistant and I were on the road, and we saw a pretty young woman, pulled over on the side. She had a flat tire, and we pulled over, and I helped her correct the flat tire, and then she gave me a little kiss after. Ed. Note: "Oh, c'mon, this clearly never happened. Lightermann, you can't even drive a car. What makes you think that we'd believe that you actually changed a young woman's flat tire, all on the side of the road?" "But it DID happened!! I do NOT lie!"-says lightermann.

Also, as a super-hero, I gave many donations to charity as well. I primarily worked for college tours. Seeing how I looked, and as a super-hero, they appreciated me. I owe them lots. One time when I went to a concert there, and everyone was very nice to me.
I was always a very strong athlete.

Act V-The Future is very Pleasant (V)

The future is very pleasant. Sometimes, all we do is lounge around. I still sometimes meet annually with that Grey Fox guy, and also that other guy, too. Herkomar's other friends and associates are also very pleasant too. And the beautiful Lady Victorian, also I quite like them, quite a bit. As we know our technology is AWESOME, nowadays. Always, we grow stronger. The world is very beautiful, sometimes. Markets are fair, and we are for winners.

Also, for notes, Herkomar finally married his girlfriend Alexia, in around the year 2068. They divorced a year later, I heard, someone says.

Oh, and apparently, I, lightermann, purchased a brand new astro-plane, on the coast. Way good.
Yeah.

additional notes:

Q: Are there any inaccuracies to Herkomar's book?

A: No, there are no other inaccuracies in Herkomar's book. All the rest of it is absolutely completely true.

Thank you, lightermann. Good-looking Germanic women adore you. –Herk.

Yes,
Sincerely,
lightermann, formerly, 'vandergaard'

Fin.

And that's the end.

'I hope you enjoyed.'-Alexia.

ABOUT THE AUTHOR:

Derek McKewan has worked in publishing for over three and half years. He spent two years studying at Vassar, and two and a half years, in, at Columbia University.

Known: Derek M. can do over one hundred fifty totally great voice impressions. And he can interpret over seven (and a half) different languages, including four programming languages, and also Olde (English) and Middle English. He even has experience translating Russian.

Also, he plays good piano, and did modeling back in college.

Originally, he resides from lower Manhattan. Thank you.

Blurb for back cover:

List of Characters

Lightermann (formerly "Vandergaard")
Grey Fox - changeling/ werewolf, Navajo Apache, 1800 pounds of pure muscle
Eiko-superfast/supersmart, super-inventor
I. Victorian- female Brit
Herkomar-their leader, speaks over 20 languages
Herkomar's daughter
Constiglione
Hanna
LeVay
Alexia
Spade (an American)

+2 or 3 additional others.

"Immortality is Yours...."

(Warning: This novel features highly light excessive amounts of adult content, adult language, and drug content.)

Genre: Adult Sci Fi/Fantasy; or Adult Sci Fi Fantasy.

Back Dedication page:

Dedication for Americans: This book has been dedicated to Matthew Knight, Chris, and Good Saint Jane.

Dedication for Germans: This book has been dedicated to Mark Ro'han, Claire Brechtenhauer, Jan Lieber, our good friend Strom Feld, and Matt, and Thom J. Kleinstadt; and all the good folks of Nuremberg.

Dedication for Spaniards: This book has been dedicated to Amy and Julio.